TUPPENNY

JULIA CUNNINGHAM was born in Spokane, Washington. She attended a variety of schools, but considers herself self-educated. Although there was a time when she hoped to be a painter or a musician, she has found that words suit her best. Miss Cunningham lived in seven states and France before settling in Santa Barbara, California where she now lives and writes.

TUPPENNY

BY JULIA CUNNINGHAM

AN AVON CAMELOT BOOK

AVON BOOKS
A division of
The Hearst Corporation
959 Eighth Avenue
New York, New York 10019

First Camelot Printing, August, 1981

The E.P. Dutton edition contains the following
Library of Congress Cataloging in Publication Data:

Cunningham, Julia.   Tuppenny.

SUMMARY: A secretive young girl arrives in a small factory
town and flushes out the guilt and hatred festering there.
I. Title.

For Tuppy again
with wings
and for Judy Taylor
who gave of grace

CHAPTER

1

I'm the one who started it all, began to tumble the walls of this terrible town. Me, Jessica Standing, the person nobody talks to because it takes me forever to answer. I stammer, I sound like an idiot. But I've learned to be quiet and I've learned to hate: my father and mother, who are ashamed of me. I hate their proud, ugly house, their money and their town, trapped in these hills. I never hated Victoria, my older sister, who ran away—though when I begged to go with her she just laughed and went.

The hill that rises above the town is a kind of watching place. When she returns I'll be the first person to see her. Sometimes I call out sounds—I gag on words—that have meanings. One is a clear beckoning to my sister. Another a crooning, an echo of a lullaby no one ever sang to me. And then there's the sound I release only when I'm hating enough to burst, a high sort of keening that is half howl and half prayer. And that's how it all began. This is not my story but the story of the person who answered my cry. Tupenny. She came and stood with me on that high hill, as though we had been there many times together.

No wind stirred the spikes of grass rising almost to her knees as though to engulf her in a greenness grayed by a storm-dark sky. Only her eyes held light. She looked down upon the little town below and I knew only too well what she was seeing. The main street was crossed at equal in-

tervals by narrower streets precisely two blocks long on each side. It was like a child's painful copy of a fish skeleton. The houses were as uniform as wooden boxes, and the curved trench of a river bordered this grim exactitude.

On a slope below was a group of blood-red buildings, one of which bore the high, white letters of my father's factory, THE STANDING COMPANY; and set in the dead center of the town within a short spread of stores was a structure of stone, a church.

She and I began to talk. Yes, talk. Not just her sentences, low and sweet and articulate, but mine, as ready and running as hers. It was as though I had been touched by magic. My stammering fled. All that she said to me seemed clear and right. I know that through everything that was to come, I was to remain a silent observer. And, when the time came, we would meet again on the hill. She loved me, this stranger, and I loved and trusted her.

Suddenly we stopped talking. A shadow the shape of wide, black wings fell upon her, staining the grass in front of her, and from it a coldness like a shroud of ice. She stepped out of its aura and looked up, searching for what must have thrown down this darkness, but the sky was all storm.

For an instant she stayed very still. A jag of lightning splintered close to her, leaving a smell of scorch.

In the next moment she led me down to my own house.

Afterward they remembered it was Friday, the morning Tuppenny appeared. Her coming was quiet, and when the front door of the gabled Victorian house opened to her, Mrs. Standing wondered how long she had waited before knocking. There was an odd ease about the way the girl stood there, almost as though the roles of stranger and

2

owner were reversed, and Mrs. Standing unconsciously smoothed her thin hair in a gesture of neatness.

"What do you want?" she asked the girl.

"Work" was the reply, and her voice was a part of her grace, low and undemanding. "My name is Tuppenny."

"Why us? Because this is the largest house in the village? We have a housekeeper." Maud Standing wondered why she felt she must explain. Who was this waifish-looking person, whose dark red hair fell straight to her narrow shoulders and whose eyes were so green they seemed to illuminate her pale face?

The girl did not respond.

"I brought her," said Jessica.

"Do be quiet," said Mrs. Standing.

"Well, come in anyway," said the rotund woman, and her hands fluttered down the buttons of her blouse as if to affirm their being fastened. "If you're hungry, we can at least give you something to eat."

Tuppenny followed her into the paneled foyer, into the heaviness of an entry dominated by a massive staircase and a chandelier of brass and crystal.

"Mrs. Bunch! Come quickly!" And as a large, starched woman hurried in from the rear of the hall, Mrs. Standing began to scold. "If you had answered the door as you are supposed to do, I wouldn't have been annoyed by this—this occurrence."

"I'm sorry, madam," said the housekeeper placidly. "What may I do for you?"

"Take this person into the kitchen and give her some lunch, after Victor and I are served, of course." But before Mrs. Bunch could direct Tuppenny out, there was a pounding of steps down the staircase and Victor Standing joined them.

"What's all the fuss, Maud?" He looked at the stranger but instead of dismissing her, he began to stare.

Mrs. Standing broke her husband's unusual silence. "Well, Victor? What's got into you? Don't know the girl, I'm sure!"

"No, but she reminds me of someone." He continued to inspect Tuppenny's worn blue jeans and gray sweater, the tennis shoes so used they were the color of clay. From her shoulder, secured by a cord, hung a reed stick lined with holes. His gaze halted at her long, relaxed hands. "That's what it is!" he mused. "She's got a shape like Victoria."

Maud moved to stand between him and the girl. "Oh, Victor, you are a fool! Every girl you see has some little resemblance to our daughter, as if all people didn't have bones and muscles and ears and feet! Why don't you give up and forget? She's been gone almost a year." Her short arms were raised as though she were going to batter down the invisible image in her husband's mind.

"Now you listen to me!" Victor replied, his voice so resonant it quivered the crystal prisms of the chandelier. "I've had enough of your comments! I'll say what I please when I please and about anybody I please!" He stalked into the next room, filling it to the high ceiling and rimming the mahogany walls with a boom of words. "That's one reason Victoria left us—your opinionated babble drove her out. If this girl wants work, she's got it!"

Mrs. Standing had followed him into the drawing room, but it was the housekeeper who spoke next from the hall, keeping her tones even. "We could use help, madam," she said. "The house is too big for me to keep tidy, what with the cooking to do."

Maud ignored her and went so close to her husband he could hear the rasp of her breathing. "You may own the town, Victor Standing," she spluttered, "with your parts factory and your three generations of money and everybody afraid to speak up because if they do they're out in the street, but you don't own me!"

Tuppenny regarded, from the threshold, the carved tables, the fat velour chairs, the china flowers that rose from oversized gilt vases, the wall-length draperies of puce velvet bordered by crimson tassels. Then she saw the photograph on the closed piano.

"Is that your other daughter?" she asked. The face in the frame—the taut, high-cheekboned clarity whose eyes, even thus reproduced, showed defiance—supplied the answer, but Tuppenny's question eased the tension.

"Only she was better looking than that," said Maud. "She had a sort of style like nobody else."

"Then why didn't you let her buy the clothes she wanted?" said Victor bitterly. "You kept her looking like a drudge. You made her look the way you made her live. Would have thought she was a maid in a third-rate motel."

"She got what she wanted from you, didn't she?" countered Maud. "That car she smashed up the first month she had it. The boarding school she was expelled from before the first Christmas. No discipline, that was your motto, and see what it taught her. At least in this house, she earned her keep!"

Mrs. Bunch, who had escaped the quarrel, now entered the room. "Lunch is served," she said, and with a slight motion of her head signaled Tuppenny to follow her.

The kitchen, square and white and immaculate, was a step from gloom into morning. Everything there had a reason and a use, from the filled glass cupboards to the smallest aluminum pan hanging from its special hook beside the stove. The round, blue table in the middle of the room was covered with yellow oilcloth and centered by a bowl of white marguerites.

"It is a pretty place, isn't it?" said Mrs. Bunch comfortably. "Used to be brown like the rest of the house and I told Mrs. Standing I just couldn't be happy in it. But we've duties to do." She began to pour hot soup into the three china cups arranged on a silver tray. "You take this in and then come back for the second course. It's fish today, fresh from our river."

Carefully Tuppenny set down the soup before the three silent people. Only Jessica looked at her. She returned to the kitchen. She watched the housekeeper arrange the fish and vegetables on gilt-edged plates, and when they were served she found that Mrs. Bunch had set two places at the round table. A glass of milk stood at her own.

"You must be hungry. Come far?" Mrs. Bunch forked into her food, still talking. "We see very few strangers here. We're off the main roads in this north country. Have to be. Something they make in Mr. Standing's factory needs security, and that's not all that bears hiding." She hesitated, her eyes suddenly introspective. "Another thing. We've got a minister and a place we call a church and the both of them give me the goose pimples."

The girl seemed caught in an intense stillness. She hadn't touched the food on her plate.

"But I'm blathering," said the housekeeper. "Eat up now. Well, as I was saying, strangers are pretty scarce. Oh, they drive through but there's not much to stop them, no motel, no attractive restaurant, just Al's Café. And nothing historic, though our valley is a pleasant one to pass through." Mrs. Bunch's glance lifted from her dish. She studied the girl across from her for a long moment. "How

6

did you happen to come? What brought you to this back-wash? Know anybody hereabouts?"

The girl's answer was brief and given almost reluctantly. "I had to come."

The housekeeper waited for more but when only silence followed the odd words, she continued. "Well, you must have walked. That much is certain. The bus doesn't arrive until afternoon."

"Yes, I walked."

Mrs. Bunch shrugged amicably. "If you want to keep your past your own, I'm not the one to pry. Don't believe in it. But this village is gossipy, so if you intend your business to remain a secret you'll have to make up something that satisfies. I like you, child, that's why I'm giving you advice."

Suddenly the housekeeper's words stopped. The smile on the stranger's face was so bright it seemed taken from the sunlight. Then the smile settled and Mrs. Bunch was able to go on talking. "I wish," she said hesitantly. She did not complete her thought.

"What do you wish, Mrs. Bunch?" asked Tuppenny.

"Something absolutely nonsensical. You see, I never had a child. We were poor, my husband and me, and we waited too long. He's gone now and that's an end to it." She folded her napkin and then refolded it. "You meet up with any unpleasantness in your travels?"

"No." Tuppenny ate the last of the potatoes. "Just the soles of my shoes. They're so thin I could feel every pebble I stepped on. Even some I didn't."

Mrs. Bunch laughed, then sobered as the buzzer sounded by the sink. "They'll be ready for dessert now. Clear the table and come back for it."

As Tuppeny collected the dishes, the isolation of the

three people, one from the other, at three sides of the table, was so complete it was as though they had not spoken once during the entire meal. But after she served the dessert and was about to retreat to the kitchen, Maud suddenly broke through. "I won't have it! I simply won't have it!"

"Won't have what, dear?" Victor said wearily.

"This girl—I don't want her around! She makes me remember Victoria."

Victor's eyes livened. "Does she, Maud? Not that she really looks like her, but I feel the same way."

Tuppenny paused to listen, though they seemed unaware of her being in the same room.

"You agree then? We'll pay her for the day and send her off?"

"No. We'll hire her."

Maud pushed the dessert aside. "You're cruel, Victor. You always were a cruel man underneath your manners."

"That's an absurdity!" said Victor, smiling. "Think what I do for my workers. There's not a factory in the country that pays better or has more benevolent employee policies. That's one reason we produce on schedule and nobody leaves. My people care. I give them the best deal going."

Maud drooped. "Oh, Victor, don't go on again about your business. I've heard it all so many times. Just tell me —if this girl reminds you of our daughter, why do you want her in your life?"

"For that very fact. I miss Victoria and I'll settle for scraps rather than nothing."

He got up, pulled down his vest, fingering the texture of the beige suede and the cut of this custom-made eccentricity, and left the house.

"Do you wish anything more, Mrs. Standing?" Tuppenny asked gently.

Maud, startled to discover her presence, half rose from her chair and then sat down again. "No! No! And I'm sorry for what you heard. But it's true. He blames me for everything and yet he never tried to guide her, to help her control her waywardness." She seemed now to be talking only to herself. "But what am I saying all this to you for? You may go."

Tuppenny walked slowly back to the kitchen.

"They didn't like my pudding," commented Mrs. Bunch. "Well, you sit down and eat it up. Might plump you out a little. I heard what they said. But you pay no attention to their differences. Do your work well, that's all that's required of you. You'll have a room of your own here and a good bed and plenty to eat." The housekeeper began to stack the china in the washer and for several moments said nothing. She turned twice to glance at the girl, who was spooning up the chocolate mousse, as if caught in an impulse to add further words. But each time she kept silent.

Then, at last, she came back to the table with a cup of coffee and settled herself in her chair. "I have to say one more thing to you, Tuppenny. If I didn't I'd be dishonest. If you've any other plan, any other idea of where to go, do it. Leave this house. I won't always be here, you know. I sleep out."

"I don't understand," Tuppenny replied.

"I don't mean that you should. But they'll drain you the way they did poor, wild Victoria and Jessica who might just as well not be here. That's all I intend to say on that subject."

Tuppenny looked gravely into the woman's eyes. There

seemed for that instant no distance of age or comprehension between them. "I'll stay," she said.

Mrs. Bunch dropped three sugar lumps into her cup. "You're an odd one," she said almost under her breath. "I've told you I like you but I wish you had never found us."

CHAPTER

~⟨ 2 ⟩~

That afternoon she had been told she might have two hours off, and when both Mrs. Standing and Mrs. Bunch had gone to their rooms, Tuppenny quickly left the house and walked down the incline of the hill that led to the village. How few trees there were among the squares and oblongs of the houses. Only bordering the river below the town had the willows and a few oaks been allowed to stand. Somehow the occasional maple and elm, their leaves turned by the approaching autumn, seemed a disturbance of color in the strict uniformity of house and sidewalk and street, as though, not being a part of the plan, they were intruders. Like herself.

She had reached the main street now and passed slowly by the grocery, the bank, the library, the two dress shops, their displays ordinary and drab, the post office, a variety store, an office building and, at the end of the short street, the one neon sign that read: Al's and Lou's Café. Eats.

She wondered where Mr. Standing's factory was and had only to look above the town to see that same group of dark red buildings she had seen from the hill. Only one thing was missing—the church. Tuppenny looked again. Two blocks from her, set back from the street with the river almost at its back, was the house of stone. Its granite grayness gave it a weight the clapboard houses to each side of it lacked. There was no steeple, no cross rising from its peaked roof, but Tuppenny could see a square, framed board in the grass before it. She walked over to read the message placed within it in removable plastic letters: Meet With Your Sins. And smaller, beneath: John Mason, Minister.

She was reluctant to enter this place she had seen from the hill and turned instead, walking quickly toward the café. Victor Standing went in just in front of her. His entrance stirred the lethargy of the four men at the counter and Victor went directly to one of them.

"Thought you reported sick yesterday, Jim," he said.

The man grimaced. "I'm better today."

"It will go on your record as unexcused absenteeism." Then Victor turned to greet Al, who was stacking clean glasses, and his wife, Lou, both behind the counter. Tuppenny had seated herself on the last stool in the rear.

"Came down for a cup of your good coffee, Cousin Lou," Victor continued, his voice warmer. He gestured toward Tuppenny. "Give the girl what she wants, on me."

Lou served him, then glanced at the stranger. "You name it," she said.

"Coffee, please," responded Tuppenny.

"You know her?" Lou asked Victor.

"Should. She's working for me and Maud now. The wife needs help, as particular as she is about dust. Imagines it, I tell her."

Lou laughed. "Better be like that than like Al here. He'd never see a mud print or a cobweb, if you put his nose in it."

Al grunted, not unpleasantly. "Wives!" he said. "What's yours giving us for dinner tonight, Vic?" The monthly custom of dinner at the big house was a condescension on Victor Standing's part and only because Lou was his very distant cousin.

"Didn't announce the menu but she said to be there by six. Anything new since yesterday?" Victor sat down at a table and surveyed the workmen. He enjoyed the awkwardness his presence caused them.

Curiosity widened Lou's small eyes as she served Tuppenny. "You've never been here before, have you?"

"She's not much for talking," interrupted Victor. "Bring me a beer, will you, Al? Walked into our house like she knew where she was going."

"Makes me think of somebody, don't know who," said Al, drawing himself a beer.

Victor slapped the table hard. "Great minds, Al! Said the same thing myself. Would it be Victoria?"

Al let the liquid slop over the rim of the mug in surprise. "Lord no! More like our Josie."

Victor burst into a guffaw that ended in a snort. "Josie? Your Josie? About as much resemblance as a goat to a sheep!"

Lou's face flushed. "I don't know what you mean by that, Victor Standing, and I don't permit any discussion of my daughter in this café!"

"Why not?" Victor's humor had shifted to irritation.

"She's a good girl. Not like some."

"Say what you mean!" said Victor, swallowing half the beer at once.

"You know the rumor as well as the rest of us," said Al. "Not that there's any proof."

"About Victoria running off with somebody? That what your wife is implying?" Victor was on his feet now, the beer forgotten.

13

"Now, Vic," placated Al, "no need to take offense. Lou's tired. She meant nothing."

"She'd better not! I'll ruin any man or woman who repeats that stinking gossip! I'll close down the factory before I'll tolerate it. Without me this town would die in a week."

Lou touched Victor's arm. "I'm sorry, Victor. But sometimes I miss Josie like a pain in my stomach, a bad pain."

Victor covered her hand with his own. "I know, Lou, I know. Seems like a curse on all of us—one daughter vanished, the other useless, and yours in an institution." He started for the door and turned back to them as he stepped into the street. "But I guess a coincidence isn't a curse, is it? See you tonight." He reached the corner and was gone.

There was a hum of comment from the four men.

"Guess he's right. No factory, no town."

"Not the first time he's said it."

"Why doesn't anybody ever leave this place?"

"Too safe maybe. Money's too good."

Al was talking in a whisper to Lou but near enough to Tuppenny so that she heard clearly. "You're a fool, Lou, bad as your daughter! Whatever made you bring up that rumor about Victoria? My God, he could snap his fingers and this café would have to close before the day was over. And tonight we're eating at his house."

"I'm sorry, Al. I really am. But something happens to me whenever I even hear Josie's name."

"And don't start that again either! We decided together to do what we did."

"Stop!" exclaimed Lou. "Stop right there! You decided—you and the minister. He talked you into it. I know he did."

Al rubbed his forehead as though it ached. "Lou, she's taken care of and we don't suffer from—" Seeing the expression in his wife's eyes, he cut off his words.

"Suffer from the shame of having a retarded child? That's what you meant to say, isn't it?"

"Lou," said Al with a sigh, "drop it!" He moved to the front of the café to talk with two men who had just come in.

Tuppenny did not stir from her stool and Lou, unaware of her nearness, was muttering to herself, "Ashamed. He always was. Ashamed of our poor, pretty daughter." Then she, too, left the rear of the café and Tuppenny was free to get up.

As she repassed the church, her right hand involuntarily grasped the reed flute that swung under her arm. And when she was well beyond it with no one in sight, she put the flute to her lips and began a song that started sad and then gradually the notes merged into a kind of dancing, of leaves in the wind, high and golden and free.

CHAPTER

⌒⊰ 3 ⊱⌒

The dinner that night went well enough, though Al and Lou were always a little intimidated by the sterling silver and the candlelight and the formality of being in the presence of a servant. Jessica had eaten earlier in the kitchen. With Tuppenny unobtrusively supplying the courses instead of the more imposing Mrs. Bunch, they found it easier to contribute to the conversation.

"We'll have our coffee in the living room," said Maud, rising from the table.

"How about a go at hearts?" Victor asked. "Might even put up a small bet."

"No gambling," said his wife. "I don't approve of it. Save that for your poker nights."

Victor laughed and nudged Al. "A very proper lady, isn't she?" He drew out a chair for Lou at the card table and sat opposite her. "Well, Cousin Lou, I've got the best partner even though I always seem to win anyway."

Al shuffled the cards. "You do, don't you, Vic?"

The larger man rubbed his hands together, pleased. "Some are born winners, some not," he remarked.

Lou, sensing Al's resentment, quickly directed a comment to Maud. "So you hired the strange girl. Does she suit you? Was in the café today and never opened her mouth."

"That's like her," said Maud as if it were a fact just realized. "Doesn't talk much and never really answers a question. But why call her strange?"

"What do we know about her?" continued Lou. By now the two men were listening. "I mean she walks into our town as bold as you please, gets herself a job at the best house and acts—" Lou waited to grasp her thought, then said nothing further.

"Finish your sentence, Lou," said her husband.

"No, it's too peculiar. Don't know what put it into my head."

"Now you've got me curious," urged Victor.

"She acts—and I know this is silly—as if she already knew us."

Al leaned his chair into a tilt and exploded with laughter. "You're the spookiest woman on earth!" he almost shouted.

"Do be careful of that chair," said Maud.

Al patted her shoulder. "If anything cracks up, it'll be me, not your furniture." His amusement diminished slowly. "Truth is, that girl reminded me of our Josie."

"Al, I've warned you—this is the second time today—that I don't want Josie talked about!" Lou's face was mottled now, her breathing short.

At that moment Tuppenny came in with the coffee tray and set it on a side table at Maud's right.

Lou looked at her piercingly. "Who are you anyway? Go on—give! I'm tired of all this talk."

Tuppenny's expression softened, ignoring the attack. "I drift," she said. Then she asked in a low voice, "Who is Josie?"

The tenderness in her tones dissolved Lou's antagonism but it was Al who responded. His eyes looked into the distance of a dream. "She was different, not like the rest of us. Sort of pink and transparent, like cotton candy. She never seemed to be able to listen very long, except to the jukebox. She'd wander off in the middle of everything. Got so's I stopped trying to reach her. Not Lou, though. She'd repeat and repeat and sometimes Josie would remember what to do next." His words slowed and stopped.

Victor sipped his coffee. "She was retarded," he said firmly. "No doubt about that."

Abruptly Lou stood up. "She *was*, always *was, was!* She's alive, not drowned in the river like the minister's girl or disappeared forever like yours! Oh, it's easy for Al to go all sentimental now he's put her away behind bars where I can't talk to her or touch her or—" She was crying now.

Maud started to rise but a hard look from Victor halted her. Al did not move.

"I'm leaving!" said Lou, rubbing off her tears. She faced her husband. "And I'll leave you, too, if you're not careful. For good!" She grabbed up her coat from the hall stand and hurried from the house. Only Tuppenny watched her go.

Al grinned, embarrassed. "She'll have calmed down by the time I get home. Every time Josie is mentioned she gets like a grizzly. Don't know why."

"I do," said Victor. "She won't accept Josie's deficiency. And," he added authoritatively, "in another sense neither do you."

Al picked up the cards and snapped through the deck with his thumb. "Yeah," he said, his attention on the cards. "It's not like your daughter. A bright girl like Victoria running off and never sending a word back home isn't the same as having a child who may be an idiot. At least we know where she is. But you have Jessica, too."

Victor cleared his throat as if to cancel out Al's words. "Jessica!" he said with scorn. "Tell you a secret, Al. There isn't a night when I don't look at that picture of Victoria. It's a sort of ritual. Foolish of me, I know, but I figure it's a kind of prayer and if I'm faithful to it she might come back. Never really knew why she left."

Maud got up, murmured an excuse to Al, and, telling Tuppenny to go to bed, mounted the stairs, her left hand gripping the banister to help pull herself up.

When she had gone, Victor brought out a bottle of brandy and poured generously. "Might as well end the evening cheerfully," he said. He sat back and folded his hands over his stomach. "Been thinking today, Al. What would happen if I closed down the works?"

Al leaned forward. "My God, you're not considering such a thing, are you?"

Victor laughed. "Not for a moment. Just like to think about it. Makes me feel like—well, like a giant."

"Maybe that's what you are," said Al with a strong swallow of brandy.

Victor stroked his paunch contentedly. "Oh, I wouldn't agree to that. But power's a funny thing, Al. Like eating chocolate cake. The more you have, the more you want, until you're greedy all the time. But let's talk about somebody besides me. You seen John Mason lately?"

"Last Sunday."

"Tell me something, Al. Do you really listen to his sermons?"

Al chuckled. "Not until he begins to shout. I never quite caught on to why you let him be the only preacher in town. Seem to remember another church trying to get going. In someone's house, wasn't it?"

"Yes, but it burned. Sort of discouraged the congregation. The people left soon after." Victor returned almost too insistently to the subject of the sermons. "I confess they scare me a little. Not what he says but the kind of excitement they start up. Think he's quite right in the head?"

"Sure. Just eccentric. And wouldn't you be if they found your daughter facedown in the river with her wrists cut?"

Victor nervously refilled their glasses. "Let's not hash that over again. Dorrie's dead and buried." He poked Al in the shoulder. "Going to run a game in the back room Saturday night?"

"Haven't missed yet, have I? Come early. Picked up some good whiskey last week but don't let on to Lou. Having no license is poison."

"Don't worry. I'm boss in this town. And, after all, you're not selling it."

"No," agreed Al with a smirk. "Not so's anybody can keep an account."

Victor emptied his glass and Al did the same. He recognized the sign of dismissal. "Good night, Victor. See you tomorrow."

Victor saw him to the door and watched him go. He did not notice Tuppenny standing near the top of the stairs, and when he had climbed them she was gone.

CHAPTER 4

The morning was still silvered by earliness when Tuppenny wiped clean the last tile in the fourth bathroom. She had been scrubbing since six and now had only the kitchen floor to do. After she had emptied and scoured the pail and wrung out the mop in the laundry room, Mrs. Bunch called her to the kitchen.

"Sit down and join me in a cup of tea," said the housekeeper. "You'll not last the day if you go on like this. Mrs. Standing will find more for you to do if she has to invent dirt where it isn't. Did the same to her own daughter. She pushed Victoria so hard she finally lost her. I saw it coming. And Jessica—well, she's no better than a shadow in the house." She set the teapot between them. "You're a good worker, Tuppenny, but why stay here? You're intelligent by the look of you, though one can't judge by what comes out of your mouth. Not a talker, are you? A store would pay better and be kinder to your back."

"I have to stay longer," said the girl.

Mrs. Bunch looked at her sharply. "Hiding from something or somebody?" She chuckled. "Don't expect an answer, not from you. Go on and drink your tea, and when you're through take a half hour off and amuse yourself. Explore the house, or if you wish, run outside. Victoria used to run into the hills. Came back with her cheeks all red and the sullen look washed out of her eyes. It didn't last long but I loved to see her as she should have been."

Tuppenny took the cups to the sink and with a half smile she tiptoed up the back stairs and went directly to the room that had been Victoria's. It was not locked. The sun from double windows shafted through the square, white space of it, highlighting the brilliant, framed print of a Tahitian landscape. On the opposite wall was a turbulent swirl of muted colors that might have been the sea on a stormy afternoon, and the third picture was simply an oblong crisscrossed by red and yellow bars. The furniture was sparse and the bed covered by a plain, white spread. Tuppenny opened the top drawer of the dresser and pulled out a purple scarf. Regarding her reflection in the mirror, she threw the scarf around her neck and over her shoulder. She bowed to her image and began the first steps of a measured dance.

Suddenly a shriek shattered the quietness.

Holding on to the doorway, her cheek flattened against the wood, her eyes wide and glassy, was Mrs. Standing. "God help me! I thought it was Victoria!" she cried. Her knees began to sag and Tuppenny hurried to support her to a chair. For a few minutes the woman simply sat, her hands in such a seizure of trembling she had to clasp them tight together.

"I'm very sorry," said Tuppenny. "I was just pretending."

"But it wasn't just the scarf!" said Maud weakly. "It was —I don't know exactly—it was her really being where you were and you gone."

"You don't want her back?" Tuppenny asked the question in tones as light as the dust motes floating through the sunlight.

"What did you say?" said the woman in a whisper.

"You don't want her to come home, do you?"

Mrs. Standing's fingers formed fists and her back straightened. "No! No, I don't! She was trouble, that girl, even if she was my own child." The words clicked, brittle and rapid, from her squeezed mouth. "She had badness in her and even the men in the town were beginning to notice her. I didn't want to see what was bound to happen and bring scandal to this house, to me and to Victor. Oh, he never saw it. Like the rest of them, he relished the wildness of her."

Then the words cut off with a jerk. Mrs. Standing got up so fast her right arm swung out and over a table, knocking a blue vase onto the floor. It smashed. She gasped. "Now see what you've made me do! Victor will be furious. He was proud of that thing, the price he paid for it! I never broke anything ever in this house before and it's your fault! You drove me to it!"

Tuppenny stayed very still.

"Victor idolized that girl! He won't even let me give her clothes away. I have to keep them clean and ready in the closet and he expects me to polish her shoes every week and now you've made me break one of her treasures!" She struck out at Tuppenny, her fingers tensed like claws. Her palm slapped stingingly upon Tuppenny's cheek and a nail left a long scratch on her chin.

She drew back and glared at the girl. "Why don't you say something? Why don't you hit me? Why don't you cry? Victoria did—she howled and then in the middle would break into a terrible kind of laughing. She hated me. Like Jessica, she hated me. She knew what I was really like. Oh, yes—she knew me!" Her anger cracked into tears. "You see she was right. I am a beast. I liked hitting her!"

Tuppenny touched the scratch on her chin with the

back of her hand. It wasn't bleeding. Then she removed the scarf and carefully folded it back into the drawer.

"Aren't you shocked?" Maud demanded. "Don't you hate me too?"

"I can't hate you," said Tuppenny.

"Riddles again! Why not? I attacked you. I hurt you. Say something!" She was almost pleading now.

Tuppenny was standing just behind a stream of light from the windows, and the brightness in front of her half concealed her figure in shadow. "Once in another time and place," she began, "I hated someone. I had befriended a fox. He showed me the secrets of his forest. My gift to him was smaller. It was food. But we understood each other. A man set his dogs on him, knowing he was tame. I hated that man for a long time. And then one night when I was wandering alone in the woods, missing my friend, remembering how it had been with him, the way he led me and turned once in a while to welcome me, I knew why the man had killed him. He hadn't understood. My fox was just a thieving, marauding animal to him, a creature to be eliminated, and I couldn't hate him any longer."

Maud backed to the doorway. "I don't understand. You've told me a story instead of giving a proper answer. As if I were the child, not you." She had regained her authority. "If you mention what has happened here, I shall deny it and dismiss you. Clean up those pieces and throw them in the garbage." She started to leave the room.

"Wait," said Tuppenny. She laid one hand lightly on Mrs. Standing's arm. "Did Victoria leave because of something you did?"

The older woman said nothing but her eyes were like agates.

"Because of something she knew about you?"

Maud's mouth seemed to freeze, and when she spoke her lips were stiff. "Why do you ask that? What do you know?" Her control split momentarily and words gushed through. "I was without love and he promised the gift of it. Instead he dragged me in the dirt twice over." With an effort she regained her reserve. "If he's told you, then he's as wrong as I was."

"Who? Who told what?"

"You get along about your business, girl. And I can tell you now, you'll not last long in my house!"

Tuppenny obeyed and returned to the kitchen.

Mrs. Bunch scrutinized her as she refilled the pail with soap and water and bent down to scour the floor. "She give you a hard time? Saw her follow you up. How did you get that mark on your jaw?"

"I was careless" was her cautious reply.

"Well, you watch out for her. Try not to be alone in a room where she is. Jessica stays clear. Oh, she's never touched me but you're different. You're the same age as Victoria and there were bad things going on here. Not that I was ever witness to them but I could tell and I heard plenty. Kept my mouth shut too. Don't approve of tale-telling."

Mrs. Bunch saw Tuppenny's face relax into what seemed to be affection, and was startled. Then when the girl continued to be silent, the housekeeper shrugged and took four potatoes from the vegetable bin. "And chatting never made the soup for supper."

CHAPTER

∼◁ 5 ▷∼

It was four o'clock before Tuppenny completed all the housework Mrs. Standing had allotted to her. The first thing she did on leaving the somber, brown atmosphere of the mansion was to squat down and rub the palms of her hands in the grass. The gesture seemed to break the connection between her and the house. She gazed up at the covering of ruffled clouds and inhaled the scent of the light wind that spiraled down from the hills behind the town.

Then she raised the reed instrument to her lips and breathed into it a melody that was somehow contrary to the grass under her feet, the sky above her. It even seemed to still the faint brush of the wind against her face. The pattern of it did not deny any of these but went beyond, as though its notes evoked another earth, another space.

At the final phrase a sudden restlessness seized her and for an instant she poised herself to race into the greenness of the slopes and keep on going until she reached whatever waited on the other side of them. Had Victoria felt this way too? Or had she walked the road until she caught up with a bus going far enough to finally have done with what had become a prison?

As she hesitated, the wingspread of a large bird crossed over her and she watched it diminish over the road into the town and away. She followed its direction but when she came to the church, she stopped.

Perched on the stone wall that surrounded the square building were two children, a boy of seven and a girl a few years younger.

"Don't go in there," said the boy.

"Don't," echoed the girl.

"Why?" Tuppenny asked.

The boy rummaged in his pocket and drew out a white pebble. He tossed it into the air and caught it three times.

"Why?" insisted Tuppenny. "What's the matter with it?"

The boy replaced the pebble. "It's locked and pocked and hasn't a clock!" he said, not looking at Tuppenny, and he poked his sister in the ribs.

The little girl giggled. "You're funny," she said.

Tuppenny leaned up against the wall beside the girl and said nothing. The sky was no longer white. A scud of stormclouds had spread it gray.

The boy hummed tunelessly for several moments. Then he spoke. "We don't unless they make us."

"Don't go to Sunday school, you mean?"

"They haven't any," said the boy.

"Wouldn't go to that either," joined the girl.

The boy slid off the wall and lifted his sister down after him. "And when it rains on Sunday we say we're sick." He offered this as if proof of his warning. Then, patiently, he added, "It's worse in there when there's no sun." He took the little girl's hand and led her down the incline toward the river.

Tuppenny called good-bye but they did not turn their heads.

She tried the iron knob on the door. Contrary to the boy's rhyme, it was not locked. Involuntarily she glanced swiftly around her to see if there was anyone on the street to witness her entry, then stepped inside.

The cold that enclosed her was dense, almost as though

it could be weighed. She moved against it, half expecting to meet a resistance, like wading in a stream. Then she very slowly pivoted in a circle—scanning the black walls lined with large paintings of exactly the same size, the green ceiling that matched the wooden pews—until her sight came to the altar. Or was it an altar? A black, square table, and on it stood two polished sticks, crudely glued together to form a cross, with a scored-out line on the cross arm instead of an image.

She looked again, this time for windows, but the paintings were where they might have been. Only behind the table was there a narrow slit for light, showing, outside, three spindly cypress trees. She felt as though she was shrinking, that each minute was devouring her. There were no saints here, no angels, no sign of belonging to God.

She turned away from the window and clutched her reed. She spoke aloud, compulsively. "The three trees must be for the Trinity." And the words had no sooner sounded than a shrill laugh scattered them.

The man, so close she could smell the sourness of his breath, loomed tall above her. In the dimness as she craned her head upward to see him, he was blocked out in angles, his jaw, his cheekbones, his socketed eyes. He seemed built from wood. She stepped back with a gasp of recognition.

"You're in all the paintings!" she exclaimed.

"How astute of you!" His mouth curved in a kind of sardonic pleasure. "Yes. You may also have noted that each is signed J. Mason. I am the artist." His glance swept the two walls. "Some are women, of course. I call them my people. But, yes, they do bear a resemblance to my own person. Perhaps because I own them."

Then his face hardened. "But who are you? What are you doing here?"

"I like churches," said Tuppenny.

"But not mine, is that it? I hear other thoughts behind what your voice says." He fingered the black stone that hung from his neck. "I hear resistance, a force that is foreign to me, and no fear. Why is that? I am not liked by the children in this village. A pity." He smiled again. "Keeps them in order. You never answered my question. What do you want here?"

Tuppenny replied with a statement. "You forgot the others—the ones who belong," she said.

"No wings, no halos, no prayer books in the pews, no—" He paused as if savoring the flavor of his thought. "No evidence of Paradise. Is that what you miss?"

Tuppenny's faint shadow, her back now turned to the one window, cast itself on the floor as tall as John Mason's height. "I expected them," she said and her tones were strong.

"And you imagine I forgot? That I was ignorant?"

"I didn't say that."

"Never mind what you said. I hear your mind. I don't know why I should explain myself to you but I will. The others would distract my congregation."

"From you?"

"What impudence!" He crossed the distance between them but Tuppenny did not stir. "You get out of here! I won't tolerate criticism, especially from a ferrety little snipe like you!"

Tuppenny moved slowly toward the door. "I know," she said, "why the children don't want to come."

He was at the entrance to anger. "I don't welcome them, that's why. We hold no Sunday school because my wife believes as I do that the very young are sinners. Later they are allowed to serve."

Tuppenny shuddered. The permanent chill of the church seemed visited now by a new coldness. She stumbled in her haste to be free of it.

The minister seized her right arm above the elbow. "Oh, no you don't! You will tell me who you are, where you came from, and why you are here in Standing."

Tuppenny looked rapidly around her, seeking escape. Fear rose around her, an invisible seepage from the concentration of eyes from the portraits, from the vacant benches, from the false cross on the altar.

She was about to struggle against the vise of his grip, when she felt herself released. But now his two long arms were extended sideways and, his eyes holding her fast, he began to lean toward her like a cross about to crush down on her.

"I was chosen," she stammered.

His arms chopped and he was convulsed with hoarse laughter. "You're as crazy as Dorrie!" he spluttered. "For a minute when I first saw you—well, never mind what I thought. Get taken often by spells, do you? She did, though we tried to iron them out of her. Well, she didn't last long and neither will you. Now get!" He pushed her toward the door and Tuppenny plunged into the sharp and welcome air of autumn.

CHAPTER

～✦(6)✦～

Instinctively Tuppenny ran to the one place that showed
lights, Al's Café. She walked through the cluster of the
five tables all the way back to the last stool at the counter.

Lou was drying plates a few feet away. She glanced at
the gleaming pallor of the girl's face. "Your hands are
shaking," she said. "You sick or something?"

"No," said Tuppenny in a very small voice. "I've been
in the church."

Lou grunted. "That's enough to spook anybody. Building belongs to the Masons. No one dares say anything
about the decorations. Right or wrong, what John Mason
does or says is what goes in this town. His wife too, for
that matter, but he gives a good hellfire sermon and we
go, Al and me, every Sunday. Pretty much have to."

"Why?" the girl asked.

The strength behind her question startled Lou. "Only
church Mr. Standing allows," she said before she thought.
Then she laughed self-consciously, as if to cover an indis-
cretion. "Get criticized in a town this size if you act different from the rest, and we need to sell our eats. But you
could use a cup of something hot. Put some pink in your
cheeks. What'll it be—coffee, hot chocolate?"

"Coffee, thank you," said Tuppenny. "But I'll have to
wait to pay you."

"That's okay." After serving her she continued to wipe the stack of plates.

"Take today," Lou went on, not bothering to notice if she had Tuppenny's attention or not. "It being Saturday we get a fair crowd towards seven. The factory people come in for beer and cards—in the back room, of course."

Two men sat at one of the tables and Lou left to take their order.

"How are you, Lou?" said the stout one.

"Just fine, Joe. You, too?"

"Be better after a piece of pie, make it apple, and coffee. For both of us. Took the early shift and we're hungry enough to eat nails."

"Won't find any in my baking," said Lou, smiling.

Back behind the counter she remarked to Tuppenny, "That's what the Standing Company delivers—electronics and hungry men." She laughed. "Say, you want to serve their pie? Then we'll call it even on your coffee."

Tuppenny took the plates from Lou and then came back for the coffee cups.

The two men watched her. "Who's the new kid, Lou?" one of them called out.

"Let her speak for herself," said the other.

"My name is Tuppenny," she said.

"That all? Well, mine's Joe and this is Harry."

Tuppenny returned to her stool and Lou went over to sit with the men.

"Not exactly a talker. Sort of pretty though. Who is she?"

Lou rested her arms on the table and admired the pie she had baked that morning. "Can't tell you much except she's working for Victor and Maud."

"A maid, that it?"

"Guess so."

The man jerked his forefinger at Tuppenny. "Don't let that missus pare you to the bone. She's not an easy woman from what I hear."

Tuppenny shook her head and a direct smile went from her to him. She glanced at the clock over the grill. It was time to join Mrs. Bunch in the kitchen.

"Got her jumping already," joked Lou. "Seems a nice girl but she must have left her words at home, wherever that is."

"No secret why that daughter of Vic's took off," said the smaller man. "Ground her down, they did. Used to see her on Sundays when I went fishing, running like a deer through the willows. Running and running as if she was powered by something too big for her. Only once saw her stop and there she lay face to the ground, flat out. Almost went to see if she had fainted, but didn't."

"Why not, Harry?"

"Had the feeling you get with a person asleep. They're so far off someplace else, they don't seem quite real. Don't want to rouse them. Know what I mean?"

"No, but that's okay," said Lou.

"Anybody ever hear of her again?" asked the fat one.

"No," Harry replied, "but the sheriff's still searching, statewide from what I picked up at the factory."

"My bet is she took up with some man. She was a looker for such a young one. Real bright, too. Took all the prizes—she and Dorrie, the minister's kid." He clapped Lou on the back. "Not like your Josie, Lou."

Lou got up as though she had been prodded and began to wipe the already immaculate counter.

"Sorry," said the man. "Didn't mean to bring up bad news."

"Al!" Lou called. "You come in here. Time I had a break." And she slammed her way to the rear of the house. Al appeared behind the counter, rubbing television from his eyes.

"Sorry, Al," repeated his friend. "Knew better."

"Yeah, Lou can't take any mention of Josie. Blew up at the Standings. Feels guilty or something, though it was me who pushed the idea of the institution."

"Sit down, Al. Get yourself a beer on us," offered the larger man. When Al had rejoined them, froth mustaching his lip, the worker went on. "Your trouble with Josie was nothing to what happened to the minister's child. I kind of pitied Dorrie. She always acted so scared."

"Downright frightened," agreed Al. "Lou thought she was a genius though maybe that was just in comparing her to our poor kid."

"At what?"

"Don't really know. Lou just kept saying she was gifted, that she could sense it like a light inside the child."

The next moment was uncomfortable. Then one of them added gruffly, "Well, that light sure got snuffed out."

Al slapped the tabletop. "What I never got over after she drowned was John Mason getting into that pulpit and giving us a sermon on the terrible fate of the suicide—the self-slayer, he called it."

"Yeah, we heard it."

"I still hear it!" said Al. "Their own child! Condemning their own child! Puts ice in your guts."

He got up. "Have to set up the back room for tonight. You two coming for cards?"

"We'll be there."

Al went first to the back bedroom, where he found Lou standing in front of the mirror, brushing her hair over and over, as if the even strokes brought her peace. He hugged her hard. "You all right, hon?" he asked.

She smiled. "I'm all right. Just a little tired maybe. Too much talk in this town, too much trouble, too much tragedy."

"Like every other place, I guess, Lou."

"Maybe, maybe not."

He kissed her briefly and then together they crossed the hall to the room which had been set up for the card games. They unfolded the felt cover to the big round table and smoothed it with the palms of their hands. "Think I'll be lucky tonight?" he said.

Tuppenny appeared in the doorway to say a thank-you to Lou and, wishing them both good-night, announced that she would let herself out.

They seemed scarcely to notice the girl's presence. Tuppenny smiled as she closed the front door quietly behind her.

CHAPTER

～❮ 7 ❯～

That evening, Tuppenny, tray in her hands, was just preparing to serve soup to the three people at the table who seemed glued in silence, when Victor Standing spoke. "Maud, I'm going to invite our new help to have dinner with us." He gestured Tuppenny to return to the kitchen.

"What for?" asked his wife. "She's not a guest here."

"Can be for one meal. She can sit to my right."

"In Victoria's place? You must be getting old, Victor—'notiony' my grandmother used to call it."

"That so? Mrs. Bunch!" he called. "Come in here and bring the silver for another setting. Tuppenny's going to eat with us." He got up and carried another chair to the table. "I miss my girl," he said. "We sit here night after night, not interested enough to look at each other, much less discuss anything. And Jess here, dumb as a stone. I sometimes even wish for the arguments Victoria stirred up. Made me mad but at least they dispelled the stagnation. Besides, it's Saturday. Ought to celebrate the end of the work week somehow."

"I expect you'll take care of that later at the café," said Maud.

"Mrs. Bunch, bring in some candles. We'll make like a party. Be civilized."

As the housekeeper was fixing the candles in the five-branched candelabra in the kitchen, she spoke in a low voice to Tuppenny. "I don't like this at all. They've got sort of set, with all this time passing since Victoria's absence, accepted their coffins—and that's what this house is, a vault—and now he slides you into their lives. I'm against it. Sorry I'm not sleeping in tonight, the way I used to. And I've tomorrow off. Promised my cousin I'd stop in and see her. But you watch it! Are you listening to me? You just watch it."

"Watch for what?" Tuppenny asked.

"You'll feel it," warned the housekeeper, the tray now filled with four soup bowls. "And when it happens, if it happens, you leave." She handed Tuppenny the tray, and a moment later Tuppenny had slipped into her place and briefly met Jessica's eyes. She waited for Maud to begin eating.

"Not hungry?" Victor prompted his wife—motionless as if hypnotized by the flicker of the candle flames. "Dig in," he ordered Tuppenny. "Can't wait forever."

The candlelight intensified the brown of the wood paneling of the walls and seemed almost to beckon the darkness from the corners of the room. Maud's pudgy face was flattened, a paper cutout with polished eyes. Then Tuppenny's face changed as though a mask of mischief were laid upon it. She mimed someone thrusting a miniature shovel into the liquid. Victor chuckled. Maud's look of unreality filled out into amusement.

"You never met our daughter, of course," Victor said to Tuppenny. "She looked like a painting, not pretty, but you had to look twice once you'd seen her. Didn't take after my wife. You'd have thought she had a different mother." He was observing Maud and smiled tightly as he saw her wince at his words. "She loved colors—red and orange and yellow—but my wife forbade her to wear them, made her too conspicuous, made her too"—he paused, taunting his wife—"too desirable."

"You stop this!" Maud protested. "It's not decent."

"She had a low voice, similar to yours, though you don't use it much," said Victor, directing his attention so exclusively to Tuppenny, no one else might have been present. "Once compared it to a cello, and Victoria laughed until she doubled over because she couldn't carry a tune. My wife wanted to make a lady out of her and had her practice the piano two hours a day or she'd lose her allowance."

Maud's spoon clacked twice against the bowl as she put it down. Tuppenny half rose to clear but Victor ordered her to stay. "Mrs. Bunch will serve the dinner."

The housekeeper brought in the rest of the meal so quickly it was obvious she intended to shorten the ceremony.

But Victor was not to be pushed. He went to the sideboard and poured himself a glass of wine, not offering it to the others. "The ladies never drank in this household. My wife believes it leads to what she so quaintly calls 'wrongdoing.' Not that her restrictions were effective. More than once we'd come back from eating with friends and find our Victoria drunk as an owl. Made a secret drinker out of her, my wife did."

Suddenly Maud broke from control and, lifting up her water glass, she threw its contents at her husband. She only succeeded in dousing two of the candles. But Victor's amusement was quenched. "Wipe that up!" he commanded Tuppenny.

Tuppenny ran to the kitchen and, returning with a towel, began to swab the table in front of Maud.

The woman jerked backward as if faced by a horror.

"She's back! I tell you she's come back! She's a haunt!" she shrieked. "She's come to torment me!" With one thrust she swept everything in front of her onto the floor. The plate smashed. The silver skidded under the sideboard. Food splotched the carpet with large blobs. She was pounding with both fists on the table.

Jessica pushed herself away from the table and, with a gasp, covered her face and rushed from the room.

Tuppenny put her hands on each side of the woman's shoulders to steady her. Maud stooped downward and in a scything motion swooped up a fork in her right hand and aimed at Tuppenny's throat.

Simultaneously Tuppenny staggered backward and Mrs. Bunch seized Maud from behind and sat her down hard in her chair. The fork clattered onto the floor.

Victor loomed huge in his fury. He gripped the edge of the table as if about to overturn it. "So that is what happened!" he yelled. "You murdered her! You murdered my daughter!"

"No!" she cried. "No! I tried! I went to her room and I fell on her with a pillow but before I could make her stop breathing, she threw me off! Maybe she hit me, maybe I struck my head on her bed, but I passed out and when I came to, she was gone, gone."

"My God! So the truth has erupted from you at last! I'm getting out of this!"

"You, too?" and her voice was strident, her mouth quivering. "Don't be a fool!"

"Oh, make no mistake, dear wife. I don't mean to give up what I've earned, my factory, my money, my fine house. Not even you. You're useful to me as a wife, no matter what you've done. Keeps scandal from the door to have a lady in residence." He laughed bitterly. "No—I'm not Victoria. I'll be back but in my own time—maybe tomorrow. But let one syllable of this go further than this room"—he glared at Mrs. Bunch—"and I'll ruin you all!" He turned to go. "And for God's sake, clean up this mess!"

The front door slammed on his exit.

Maud was now huddled beneath the table as if she could hide from herself in its shelter. Her crying brought no tears, just harsh gasps so close upon each other Mrs. Bunch covered her ears with both hands. It was Tuppenny who fell to her knees and enclosed the agonized woman in her arms. She said nothing, simply held her.

Gradually the woman's dry sobs ceased. For a long time she rested where she was and then, at last, she straightened and allowed Tuppenny to help her to her feet. For an instant she clung to the girl, looking into her eyes as if listening to something unspoken.

The instant passed and Tuppenny released her. "I loved Victoria. I loved her and I didn't want her to turn out like me, a wicked, crazy old woman. But I tried the wrong way. I tried to make her gentle, to crush the passion from her. And all I did was drive her out." Her voice was weak and low, her breathing shallow. "But do you know what she said to me once? Oh, yes, I knew she was going. Me and nobody else. She said, 'I'm going for your sake, mother.'"

"What could she have meant by that?" asked the housekeeper wonderingly.

"I never knew." Maud turned again to Tuppenny. "Go," she said, her voice now threaded with strain, but clear. "Go, child, whoever you are. Go now. You won't have to worry about me. Nobody will. Not anymore. I'm rid of what poisoned me."

Tuppenny glanced toward the housekeeper. Mrs. Bunch nodded. "I'll take care of her," she said. She kissed Tuppenny lightly. "Do as she says. It's best."

CHAPTER

~⟨ 8 ⟩~

Tuppenny paused outside the café and looked through the steamy window. All the tables were taken and the sound penetrating into the frosty night was loud and laughing. She went in just behind two tall men who made their way directly through and into the back premises where the noise was even greater. Tuppenny found Lou at the rear of the counter, tossing and salting fried potatoes. She waited until she became aware of her.

"Mrs. Herd, could you give me a job in exchange for room and board?" she asked.

Lou wiped her hands in a towel slowly and thoroughly. "Why? Maud kick you out? Not surprised. If she can't run a person's life, she hates them. Don't know why." She scanned every detail of Tuppenny's appearance. "Scratched you, did she?"

Tuppenny did not reply to her question. Instead she smiled, saying, "I believe Mrs. Standing has changed."

Lou felt momentarily lost in studying Tuppenny's face, unable to look away from her eyes. "Funny thing," she murmured almost inaudibly. "Like my Josie." Then she wiped her forehead with the back of her hand as if to disperse her dreaminess. "I mean she was tender too. Most times, that is. Once in a while she bit down on some little thing of no importance to anyone else—like the day a mouse got his leg ripped off by a trap we set—and she'd spit and yell. But it never lasted long. I'd take her to her room and sing to her. That stopped the fit. She'd listen and forget. But what am I telling all this to you for? None of your business. Anyway, she's shut up for good now. Best thing, Al said."

"You mean she's in a hospital?" Tuppenny prompted.

"Not exactly. In a home where they keep watch on the feebleminded. Used to visit her regularly but gave it up. She just turned her back on us like she never saw us before. Didn't cry. Just turned her back. I used to be sick all the way home, so Al put his foot down and I can't go anymore."

"Hey, Lou, how about another beer?" someone called from the center of the room.

"Yeah, Lou," joined another, "the service is slow as snails tonight."

"Okay," Lou answered. "I'm coming." She beckoned Tuppenny around the counter. "Wash up those glasses first. There's plenty for the two of us to do."

A few minutes later a hail of respectful greetings heralded the last one in, Victor Standing.

"The wind too rough?" asked the foreman of the factory.

Victor smoothed his hair. "Took a long walk," he commented. He waved to the crowd, then spied Lou. "Al got a game going?"

She pointed toward the back room. Victor smiled at Tuppenny as he passed her. "Got yourself a new job, I see. Good thing, too." His expression was bland, as if he had completely erased what had happened a half hour ago in his own home. He vanished into the rear of the house and Tuppenny heard another rise of voices.

Within an hour the café was packed, all the tables taken,

and the men and some women two-deep at the counter. Lou cooked while Al drew the beer and poured the soft drinks. Tuppenny served, cleared, and when she had a few minutes, washed the dishes.

Only once did Al speak to her, and that was to tell her to keep out of the back room. And it was Lou who explained, in a whisper, that Al let them drink hard liquor during the poker games although they had no license and would lose the café if they were found out. "Not that the police don't know it," she added. "But they win most nights."

At ten-thirty, except for the gamblers, the outer room was only half-full, and both Lou and Tuppenny sat down at the counter to rest. Lou had just let out a long, tired sigh, when a tall woman, so thin her purple wool dress hung from her like drapery, came up beside her.

"Good evening, Lou," she said.

"Jen? Never thought to see you here on Saturday night!"

"Nor did I," countered the newcomer.

"What can I do for you?"

The minister's wife pursed her tiny mouth. "Can you bake me three apple pies for tomorrow afternoon? John is having a supper meeting after services and you know how he is—doesn't permit me to cook on a Sunday. Just told me he needed them."

Lou shrugged. "Okay, Jen. Let me see if I have enough apples."

Tuppenny caught the woman staring at her with distaste. "Never saw you in Standing before. You a relative of the Herds?"

"No. I work here."

"Since when?"

"I only started today."

Silence grew, weedlike and spiny, between them.

"Coming to church tomorrow?" Jen asked.

"If I'm wanted there" was all Tuppenny offered.

The woman laughed rustily. "Not a question of wanting, is it? Where you ought to be."

"If that's what you think, I'll come."

The minister's wife flexed her long, delicate fingers that were somehow contradictory to the severity of the rest of her. "Why should you care what I think?" she said. Her voice attacked. "You're a stranger to me and likely to remain one."

"I do care," said the girl.

"Do you? Well, find someone else to concern yourself about. I'm the minister's wife and I do a good job of being that. For the rest I'm old and I'm ugly." She laced her fingers over her mouth as if shocked at what was coming from it. Then, self-consciously, she resettled herself into her former primness. "I just don't mix with people," she added, shutting off any tenuous connection that might have momentarily existed between them. But one more sentence squeezed past her rejection of this strange girl beside her. "Not since Dorrie."

Lou had just returned. "Why, Jen," she said, "I've never heard you speak your daughter's name, not ever, not since the river got her."

Jen stood up. "You can do my pies?"

"Yes, Jen, I can. Have them ready before church. I'll send Tuppenny over with them."

"I'll pick them up myself." With that she left the café.

Lou let out a whoof of breath. "I'll be blessed!" she exclaimed. She looked at Tuppenny. "You bewitch her or something? She's been as responsive as a stone on the subject of her daughter. Everybody quit long since trying to tell her they were sorry."

"What was it?" asked Tuppenny.

Lou checked the room to see if anyone needed service, then relaxed. "That Dorrie was all twisted up inside. Nothing wrong with her brain. She and Victoria took all the prizes at school, and her teacher said she had filled fifteen notebooks with poetry. Nobody ever found them after it happened, though. But she was twisted. Never hardly spoke and acted all hidden sort of, though she and Victoria were rumored to be real chums. Some blamed John, said his insanity infected her. Drowned herself in the river the day before Easter. Last year." Lou's surprise renewed. "But that Jen—she never even listened when we tried to comfort her. Only smiled very small like she hurt inside and didn't want to let it out."

"Tell me about Victoria," said Tuppenny quietly.

"I liked the girl, wild or not. Never acted wild around me. Funny though, I used to wonder why she was so different from Victor and Maud. Almost like she was someone else's." Then Lou laughed at herself. "Al says my imagination is bigger than my sense. Might be right."

"When was it she ran away?"

"Come to think of it, just a couple of days after Dorrie died." She looked at the girl across from her. "But why did you want to know about Victoria? You're not likely to meet up with her, you or anybody else."

Tuppenny turned away from Lou's gaze. "I feel as though I knew her."

"That comes from living with the Standings. Best forget what you can't help is what I try to live by."

There were no more questions, and a companionable silence joined the two of them.

It was midnight before the door closed on the last person. Al was straightening the back room while Lou stacked glasses and gave the grill a final cleaning. Tuppenny, her head on her arms, was asleep at the middle table.

Al came in, smiling. "A good night in there. How about here, Lou?"

"Made a fortune," Lou joked.

"The girl still here, is she?"

"Tired out. She really works, Al. Never stopped once."

"Okay. She comes cheap, I'm sure. We'll keep her for a while. But no promises. Agreed?"

"She's cheap enough," said Lou. "Only asking room and board."

"Better show her where her room is. Never got much comfort from a tabletop myself. Giving her Josie's?"

"Where else?" Lou joggled Tuppenny's left arm. "Wake up, hon," she said. "We're all beat. Takes a couple of days to get over Saturday night."

Tuppenny was instantly alert and followed Lou into a tiny room that looked onto the back porch.

"I'll get some bedding for you. Didn't have a chance to neaten it up for you. Haven't been in here myself since Josie went."

Left alone, Tuppenny looked at the bareness. Except for a dresser, a partially broken wicker chair, a mirror and a bed, it might never have been inhabited. It was filled by an atmosphere of abandonment. The dead potato vine in a grimy jug and two postcards stuck into the edges of the speckled mirror only accented its forlornness. The one relief was a photograph of a rose that had been taped to the wall opposite the bed. Somehow it seemed to have escaped the dust that should have filmed it.

"Sort of dreary," commented Lou as she came in with

sheets and a blanket, and began to make up the bed. "But you can freshen it up tomorrow. I'll lend you a vase. There are some marigolds in the backyard."

The two of them finished the bed making, and with a brief "Good night," Lou closed the door on the room's new tenant.

Tuppenny went to the window and, wiping a circle in the center of the glass with the palm of her hand, she gazed out at the night. She looked toward the stars, then picked up the little reed pipe and played a tiny song as brief as a breath.

CHAPTER
9

The next morning Tuppenny awoke first to the smell of coffee, then to the unusual somberness of the room, and last, to a knocking on the door.

"Get yourself out in five minutes!" It was Al. "There's plenty of mopping up to do before church."

Tuppenny hurried into her clothes, doused her face in a basin of cold water, and rubbed herself dry so roughly she was completely awake as she joined Lou in the café. Lou had set a glass of milk and a stack of buttered toast on the counter for her.

"No need to yell, Al," she was saying. "Sounded like you were talking to Josie."

"Yeah," he assented grumpily. "Forgot. Used to have to tell her every little thing ten times over." He swallowed his coffee steaming hot as he inspected the café. "Come to think of it, Lou, never heard you mention Josie like you're doing now." He glanced at Tuppenny. "Ever since our new help. What's your name again, girl?" He rapped on the counter with his knuckles, his impatience causing a frown.

"Tuppenny."

"Damned queer name. What's it stand for?"

Lou took up the answer. "It's a very tiny coin."

"Never heard of it."

"English," added Lou.

Al slapped the counter, making Tuppenny's milk glass jiggle. "That right? Well, get your English airs busy clearing up last night's mess, if you can manage it."

Lou signaled to Tuppenny, beckoning her toward the back of the house. Tuppenny waited while Lou extracted a broom and dustpan from the hall closet; then they both entered the card room. The air was thick with the smell of cigar butts and the stale splashes of whiskey still coating the bottoms of the glasses. Lou gathered up the clutter of beer bottles from under the card table. "Pay no attention to Al," she said. "He's cross today. Usually is on Sundays. Tired, I guess. Get a tray from the front and just stack the glasses behind the counter. I'll tend to them. Then sweep out last night. Might begin by opening the windows." She left the room.

While she worked, Tuppenny could hear conversation in the café.

"Al, did you put away the cards and chips?" Lou was saying.

"Think I'd forget that?" he asked sarcastically. He was peeling potatoes and nicked his thumb with the paring knife. "Damn! What comes of useless questions."

When Al had locked himself into the bathroom, Tuppenny rejoined Lou.

"That all the clothes you have?" asked Lou. "Well, they're clean enough anyway." And when Tuppenny stood silent before her, Lou added, "You want to ask me something?"

"Do I have to go?"

"To church? You sure do—that is, if you want to stay in Standing. We all go—the worst and the best of us— no work in the factory and, for us, no customers."

"Does Mr. Standing insist?" asked Tuppenny quietly.

Al came in, buttoning his shirt. "Too many questions from the help."

"Won't hurt to tell her," said Lou. "Yes, Victor made the law and John Mason enforces it. The answer is yes, you have to go." Lou gazed through the front window at the stolid square of stones across the street. "Sort of peculiar though, isn't it?"

"Isn't what?" asked Al in an irritated tone.

"How John decorated the inside of his church. Jen says they're supposed to be people around here, sort of pictures of the congregation, but I never saw any of them on our streets."

"Made them up probably," said Al. His face smoothened as he saw two women and a man heading for the café. "Saints, maybe."

"No," said Tuppenny so positively Lou looked at her, surprised. "They're not saints."

"Have it your way," muttered Al. He greeted the three people by name and brought them coffee.

"I agree with you," said Lou. "More like ghosts. But I've got to freshen up. You help Al, if he needs anything. Jen's pies are behind the counter."

An hour later, Jen having come and gone, the three of them, preceded by the customers, crossed the street to the church. A whirl of unexpected wind spiraled up their legs and Tuppenny shivered.

Lou noticed. "You'll be needing a coat pretty soon if you stay here. That all you've got—what's on your back?"

Tuppenny nodded and held the door for the five of them. She let the others go ahead and seated herself in the back row. What was the half-sweet, half-spoiled smell that permeated the building? Did the riverbed send up such odors or was there a dead rat beginning to rot under the floorboards? The door to her right swung open as the people entered, blending a little autumn into the air, partially dispelling the basic stench. Tuppenny breathed deeply each time and then forgot her distress because the stout woman who had just plumped herself down beside her canceled all else with her violet perfume.

Then Tuppenny looked at the portraits. The eyes of each one were directed toward the pulpit. Round and flat, they stared in permanent attention. At that moment the minister ascended the platform and waved his right hand to the back of the church. Three voices from the tiny choir loft above her quavered into a tune without words, unaccompanied. The pitch became so insecure, the balance of the voices so uneven, all semblance of a melody vanished and the sound became a kind of whining. It finally wavered raggedly to a conclusion.

John Mason was robed in black and from his neck hung a chain of square silver links. Instead of a cross, at the end of it hung a hollow triangle centered by an eye. Was this what the portrait people were focused on? Tuppenny bowed her head, expecting a prayer, but she soon raised it again because the minister had begun to speak. His voice was strangely small, as though it were issuing from a pipe the width of a straw in his throat, and his words were enunciated so close to his teeth, a slight hissing underlay them.

"Each of you has come to offer tribute in some form or other: your time, your money, your thoughts, your worries and even—" He paused and, gripping the edges of the pulpit, leaned forward. "—your sins."

Tuppenny felt a cut of autumn air across her ankles. The wind had pushed the door open a crack. Or was it someone outside, listening?

"Yes," his mouth was held now in the form of a smile, "even your sins. And you must lay them on this altar with pride, for they are part of you and, like the entrails of the goat in ancient days, they must be torn from you and scrutinized and, finally, given as a gift."

A sound like the thrumming of a drum started up behind Tuppenny, as though something were trying to buffet down the stone walls of the building. Then she heard the rattling of what must have been a whirl of dead leaves.

"A gift to whom? you may be asking yourselves." The minister raised both arms above his head. "A gift to me, your shepherd and your host! Come forward, my children! Come forward and choke up the darkness that dwells in each one of you!" His exhortation grew so shrill that Tuppenny plugged her ears and simply watched. As he spoke, one by one in what became a slow procession, the people obeyed him as if mesmerized, until almost the entire congregation was in the aisle. Just as the first few pressed against the pulpit, John Mason descended, turned, and began singing in a high hum as he led them toward and through a low door to the left of the altar. All around Tuppenny the rest were singing too.

A woman tapped her on the arm, indicating she was to follow her. She whispered, "It's the River Song," and resumed the near monotone of notes.

As Tuppenny, the last to leave, stepped into the tempestuous morning, she was almost thrown to the ground by the blowing of the wind. But what she witnessed stiffened her.

Jen Mason had been waiting by the river's edge and her body had taken the shape of a crooked cross. Beyond her the water rushed and curdled and slapped itself on the banks of earth and grass, seemingly joined to the forces that were being urged by the minister and his ecstatic wife. The humming had ceased.

Then the man expelled from his lungs a long cry like the bleat of a sheep. Jen's arms dropped to her sides and she bowed her head. The communion, whatever it had been, had taken place. It was over.

The people turned from the river and dispersed, leaving only the man and woman still contemplating the turmoil of wind and water.

Tuppenny suddenly about-faced and ran as hard as she could from the churchyard and across the street to the protection and warmth of the café. And when she stood in the center of the smells of coffee and bread and bacon beginning to fry, she breathed so deeply she coughed.

"What's the matter?" asked Lou. "Our Sunday craziness scare you?"

"Not exactly what you'd call regular services," commented Al, whose humor was restored to normal. "Wonder what he does with our sins once he has them."

"Best not to meddle with such thinking," said Lou. "Best not."

CHAPTER

❧ 10 ❧

At two o'clock, with Al napping and Lou reading in the vacant café, Tuppenny went to the room where she had slept the night before, made the bed and attempted with a dust cloth and a broom to reduce its aspect of disuse and desertion. But even after she had cleared the mirror of film and eliminated the smell of dust, it held no warmth, no welcome.

She was just ready to return to the café, when she heard a light and timid knocking at the back porch door. She tiptoed down the hallway, past the room where Al lay asleep, and carefully turned the knob.

There stood Maud Standing. Her hair was disheveled and she seemed smaller than Tuppenny remembered her, as though she were bound around by invisible strings.

"Let me in, child." Her voice was tight and tiny. "Tell Lou I'm here but don't tell Al. I have to talk to Lou. Right away."

"Al's in his room," Tuppenny replied. She pointed in toward the café. "Lou's alone in there."

Maud almost ran into the front room. "Lou! You've got to listen to me!"

"Take it easy, Maud. Tuppenny, you pour her a cup of coffee and give each of us a couple of fresh doughnuts. Take one yourself."

When she had served the two women, Tuppenny started to seat herself on a stool.

Maud's hands fluttered distress. "No! I have to talk to you alone, Lou!"

At a nod from Lou, Tuppenny retreated to the back premises.

"Odd girl," murmured Lou. "I like her."

"But that's what I came about," said Maud, coughing on a lump of doughnut too hastily swallowed. "We want her back." She cut off Lou's response with the hurry of her words. "Victor says it's all right with him if we have her and he's promised to send her to school and get her some new clothes and whatever else she needs and I'm going to fix her up a nice room all her own and—"

Lou pressed her hand firmly on the other woman's arm to calm her. "Relax, Maud. You're all flushed."

Some of her nervousness simmered off. "You see, Lou," she said more slowly, "Mrs. Bunch needs assistance with the housekeeping and she says the girl is very efficient and—" Suddenly tears welled in her eyes. "Lou, the truth is I'm lonely. Since Victoria left I seem to need her—the way she was before she was old enough to scold and discipline. Somehow I had to hate her, my own daughter, when she began to be different from me. I mean she liked peculiar paintings and colors my mother would never have allowed in the house and she even used to sing crazy songs, songs with ugly words to them, vulgar words, and I was left out somewhere far away so I had to hate her. But I know now I didn't. I was afraid she hated me. It was love turned around backwards. Oh, I know you think I'm crazy, everyone does. But now now. Not since—"

The cut into silence lasted so long Lou interjected, "Since what, Maud?"

Maud looked down at her pudgy hands. "I can't tell you that but the change came when that strange girl walked in on us. Please, Lou, please. Give her back!"

Lou was frowning. "But, Maud, she's not mine or Al's or yours or Victor's. Nobody can trade her back and forth like a sack of grain. She's free and can go where she pleases. Like her coming into this town all by herself from God knows where. She can quit all of us tomorrow if she wants. She came to us because it was her choice. I don't know why, and I realize now how much I've needed help here in the café for a long time, only Al was too stingy to hire and he never even let Josie try." Lou's sentences accelerated so fast it was now *her* face that had reddened in her earnestness. "Said she was too stupid to learn. When I'd get her alone we'd repeat and repeat the same thing over and over and finally she understood and did it right. But the minute Al was watching she'd drop the dish she was wiping or spill what she was pouring or, sometimes," Lou's voice broke a little, "sometimes she'd just stand and cry."

Maud's hands covered both of Lou's as if to transfer reassurance, but Lou was not even aware of her touch.

"I never wanted to send Josie away. It was Al. He said she had to go. And now she's rotting in that awful place!" Lou was glaring at the person facing her, as if it were not Maud but Al. Her tones had become strident. "No! You can't have Tuppenny! She's—she belongs here—with me!"

The other woman pulled herself out of her chair heavily, as if she had aged twenty years. She had lost, but the remnants of pity in her made her say "But Lou, she isn't Josie, you know." She left the café, letting the door swing loose after her.

Tuppenny re-entered the room.

"Al!" Lou was calling. "Come in here. Tuppenny, you get me my hat and coat."

A moment later Al's sleepiness dropped from him as he saw Lou shrugging into her rough, green overcoat.

"I'm taking the rest of the day off," she announced, pulling her felt hat down clumsily over her head.

"You're what?" Al's astonishment was loud. "You know how Sunday evening is—busy as hell." He laughed uncertainly. "Shouldn't say that, I guess—not today."

Lou went to the door. "I mean it, Al. I'll be back by the midnight bus. You stay away from the cards tonight. Without me up front you won't have time to amuse yourself. And no drinking."

He grabbed her sleeve. "By damn, you'll tell me where you're going! I'm the boss here." He shook her.

Lou simply stood solid. "Can't you guess?" she said. "Or are you still trying to hide from yourself what you forced me to do?"

He released his hold on her. "You're not going to visit Josie? Lou, you can't. You said you never wanted to see her again after we decided. You can't go back on that."

"I can and I am" was all she said as she walked rapidly out and into the howl of the wind.

Al stomped into the back of the house, and Tuppenny was left to take orders for pie and coffee from a man and woman who were seating themselves at the counter. She had just cut the slices when Al returned, muttering, "No drinking, she said? First and last time that woman gives me orders! I'll teach her!" He turned on Tuppenny. "You keep hopping or I'll put you out. Maybe I fathered an idiot, but now it seems I married one, too!" He disappeared into the back.

The next hours were so busy for Tuppenny that even

her increasing tiredness was not real to her. Not until at last the people had gone to their homes and except for one young boy the café was empty. Even the card room was vacant of players. She lifted a frying pan to pour out the grease and her grip slipped. When the hot fat hit the grill, a flame a foot high flared toward her. She grabbed two towels and tried to beat it down, but not before it had touched and caught on the window curtains above the stove.

"I'll get help!" the boy shouted and darted from the café.

A draft from the rear entrance fanned the fire.

"Oh, my God!" It was Al. His speech was blurred. "It's a judgment on me! It's everything I have burning to nothing!" He staggered and fell against the counter, knocking a row of glasses onto the floor. They splintered in every direction. He threw a kettle of hot water at the curtains but missed the fire. "Josie!" he yelled. "Got to save Josie!" He crashed through the hall and into Tuppenny's bedroom. She heard two hard thumps and knew he had fallen.

Abandoning the crisis in the café, Tuppenny ran to where he lay, half-stretched over the sill of the doorway. She knew it wouldn't take long for the flames to find their way through the entire house and, thrusting her hands under his armpits, she heaved him, one foot at a time, onto the back porch.

At that moment people poured into the front room, the minister leading. "Nobody here?" he called. "Jen, you fill whatever you can find with water, and the rest, douse it on—fast!" In three minutes there were only the last curls of smoke spiraling up from the blackened windowsills and the wall behind the grill.

John Mason sat down. "Can't figure why the place is empty."

"It isn't," said Tuppenny from the doorway. "I'm here."

"Then where the devil were you a few minutes ago? Afraid of fire?" He seemed to enjoy the accusation.

"I was in the back."

"Sleeping, no doubt. Where're Al and Lou?"

"Lou has gone visiting," the girl answered.

"And Al?"

"He's gone, too."

"Funny thing to do," commented the minister. "Why didn't they close up?"

"I'm here."

The man laughed without humor. It was a metallic sound. "And a very responsible person you turned out to be." He got up. "Well, let's go. The girl can busy herself cleaning up and think herself lucky there's anything left to clean."

The group left almost as quickly as they had come, and Tuppenny had just time to sponge out the water and wipe the floor when Lou appeared from the night.

She looked once at the charred wall, then at Tuppenny, and all she said was "Accidents happen." But as she took off her coat and hat, she gasped. "Where's Al? He all right?"

"Yes. But I can't get him to bed without you helping."

"Drunk?" Lou sighed. "I sort of thought that might happen after our quarrel and I shouldn't have gone, I guess. But I'm glad I did. Well, come on, let's get the old man under the covers and let him snooze it off."

While they struggled with his dead weight, Tuppenny told Lou about the minister and that she had concealed the fact that Al was where he was and how he was.

Lou smiled. "You're a good friend to us, Tuppenny. I'm grateful." Kissing the unconscious man on his forehead, she and Tuppenny went into the hall. "You get some rest yourself," she said to the girl. She glanced into Tuppenny's room. "We'll have to get busy and fix this up pretty," she said, and Tuppenny sensed she didn't mean to do it for her.

CHAPTER

~◄ 11 ►~

When Tuppenny came into the café the next morning, Al was there before her. He gave her no greeting but went on prying off the scorched boards of the inner wall. It was not until she had drawn the hot water, preparing to scrub the counter, that he spoke, his voice as noncommittal as his face. "Lou says I owe you."

"I don't know what you mean," Tuppenny replied.

He turned halfway around. "I don't remember but she says you got me free of the fire." Her smile erased his embarrassment. He looked straight at her now. "You don't seem strong enough to move an armchair, much less a hulk like me. How'd you manage it?"

"I had to," said Tuppenny.

"Well, I'm grateful to you." He slammed his hammer against the last charred sliver and it broke away from the wall. He began scraping at the lathing.

"And that's not all," said Lou, coming in with a hug for Tuppenny on the way. "When John and the rest of them came in to put out the fire, she said you were with me, not stretched out drunk on the back stoop. You can add a few thank-yous for that too."

"Yeah? Well, she knows. I said it already. Reason I had a few too many was I was mad at you for going to see Josie without any warning, any discussion with me."

Lou was mopping the floor and said nothing.

Al gathered the ripped boards in his arms and, passing his wife, grunted at her, "How is she?"

One word answered him. "Puny."

"Meaning what?" asked Al. He tossed the wood into the rear hallway.

Lou stopped working. "I mean just that. She's withering, Al, withering in that dump. She sits on the floor all day and eats with her fingers out of a bowl because nobody bothers to give the kids knives and forks to eat with." She gripped the mop handle and swung it energetically back and forth across the same space, unaware of the repetition. Her head was lowered but both Tuppenny and Al knew she was crying.

For an instant Al's eyes closed over his confusion. Then he marched back to the burned area and began digging at the lintel of the window. The nails squealed as he loosened the ledges. He spoke over the noise, deep and clear. "First thing after I get this wreckage repaired I'm going to paint that back bedroom. Maybe you could make some decent curtains and put a rug in there to cover the cracks in the flooring. Needs a new dresser, too, and a comfortable chair. We'll pick them up secondhand. What do you say, Lou?" He sneaked a look behind him.

Lou ceased the motion of the mop. "For Tuppenny?" she asked. "She deserves it."

"No, Lou. For Josie. I owe her, too."

"Oh, my God!" The mop handle clattered downward. Lou rushed around the counter and put out her arms to hug Al.

He shoved her off. "You want to reopen by tomorrow night or next Christmas?" he asked. "Then get to it. Both of you."

62

"But when can I—can we—go get her?" said Lou, still not quite believing.

"Tomorrow afternoon. I'll borrow Victor's car. It makes better time than mine."

This time he could not repulse her. She encircled him with both arms and kissed him all over his face. He pretended to fend her off but ended by returning her embrace.

With a last kiss they went back to their tasks and it was not until the café was shining again, except for the scars of the fire, that Tuppenny made her announcement.

"I'll be leaving."

"Oh, no!"

"But you just came!"

Tuppenny smiled. The three were still for a moment. Then Lou asked, "But where will you go?"

"Just away," Tuppenny answered, "unless something stops me."

Lou began to laugh. "You're about the most mysterious creature I ever hope to meet, though I'm sure I'll never meet anyone like you again. But that's okay. You've a right to keep private. But tell me one thing, Tuppenny. I'm curious. How old are you?"

"A hundred years and a day."

Now Al was laughing too. "See, Lou, what you get for your curiosity? Leave the child alone. She knows what she wants. That was the trouble with Victor and Maud. Never let their Victoria off the leash. No wonder she broke it. Would have done it myself, had I been the girl."

Lou pinched him affectionately. "Any time you can think like a girl I'll—I'll eat a week's doughnuts in one sitting."

"It's true," he insisted.

"Well, you tend to your own affairs. It's happier that way. And besides, we'll have our Josie to help us and that's enough." Lou's eyes seemed to accumulate brightness. "Oh, Al, she's going to be so happy being home! Once she gets used to us again."

And as Lou's voice filled the café with this spill of happiness, Tuppenny backed, unnoticed, into the hall and out the rear door. She paused before the church, reached out one hand to turn the door handle, then, shaking her head as if in answer to some inner instruction, walked down the road the way she had come into the town.

The morning was pure gray, the hills such a subdued green they seemed dyed in the overall monotone. But between the motionless trees and the sky was a halt so definite it created an expectancy, a tension that even the stir of one blade of grass might explode into storm. Tuppenny's footsteps were soundless on the pebbled dirt of the road.

Then she saw someone approaching as though risen from nowhere. Nearer and nearer until the image became distinct.

A tall, dark girl confronted her, blocked her way. "You going, me coming," she said. "You might be the same person I was a year ago. Might be me."

At the start of her voice the first fingers of wind brushed down from the hills.

That was when Victoria came back—and I was there watching. I saw her coming and knew Tuppenny would recognize her.

CHAPTER
∽ 12 ↦

"You're Victoria," said Tuppenny.

Defiance deepened the girl's voice. "Victoria Standing," she said. "And who are you?"

"I worked for your family." Tuppenny seemed to be listening to something beyond this bitterness.

Victoria made a sound like laughter. "Did you? How many scars did you come out with? Oh, I'm not talking about whiplashes or anything that honest. Just cuts on your insides. I'm seamed with them." She slowly started to walk toward the town, Tuppenny with her.

"Then why are you going back?" was all Tuppenny asked.

"Necessity. Money. I'm a Standing after all and entitled to my share of the profits from the factory. I've earned it, don't worry. Not fitting rifle sights, but in that damned house. I'm a member of my father's empire and I've contributed my taxes in sweat and servitude." She seemed to relish each sentence and her stride lengthened. "Yes, for money, and for another reason that I'll take care of in my own way."

Tuppenny looked at the proud, angular profile, as proportionate as an ancient French stone carving and as alien as it was beautiful. In no other person in Standing had she seen a similar line of cheek or jaw, or any echo of the wide, dark eyes, certainly not in Victoria's parents.

She then saw that the girl's fists were clenched. They were passing the church.

Victoria halted. "This building is going to fall," she said, with a kind of satisfaction. "But not yet. You know this charming couple, John and Jen Mason?"

"Not really," Tuppenny replied. "Why?"

Victoria gazed for a full minute into Tuppenny's eyes, judging, deciding. A small, first smile formed on her mouth. "I like your looks. You're different, like me." She touched the little reed pipe that dangled from Tuppenny's shoulder. "I bet you play secrets with that. Tell you what. I'll buy us a couple of sandwiches at the café and we'll have a picnic by the river and talk."

Lou's welcome to Tuppenny showed plainly how much she already missed her. "But I thought you were gone forever!" she exclaimed. "Coming back to us?"

Victoria stayed behind her companion.

"No, thank you, Lou," Tuppenny replied. "But could we have two sandwiches to take with us?"

Lou grinned. "Seeing as it's you I'll let you make them on the house. Whatever you want." She looked now at the second figure. Her face blanched. Her left hand went to her heart. "You're—you're—" She couldn't seem to expel the name.

"Yes. It's me. The stray lamb, the black one."

"Al!" Lou called for her husband as if for help. "It's Victoria come back! Victoria Standing!"

"No need to call out the troops," Victoria commented, her ease so complete it was grace.

Al pounded into the café from the rear. "Glad to see you back," he said. "And won't Victor and Maud be in a state of shock!"

"Won't they though." Victoria made no move to join

Tuppenny behind the counter where she was putting two cheese sandwiches together. "Anyway, I'm only here for a short visit, very short, if all goes as I wish it."

"They'll be glad to see you." Lou threw her words against the girl's sarcasm.

"Will they? Like you'd be glad to see Josie and the Masons to see Dorrie? I think not."

Lou sighed. "You've not changed, Victoria. You like to hurt. And why bring up Dorrie? She's dead."

Tuppenny was now beside her but Victoria was encircled by aloneness. "I'll tell you why. I loved her. She was my true friend, the only one I ever had or ever will have." The force from her now was passionate. "She became like the wild things who knew her—the foxes and the deer and all the creatures who flee from anyone not clean of ugliness. She could coax them out of the trees and meadows and they stood around her as freely as wild flowers. She stopped speaking, except to me, because whatever she said they punished her for. She was so bright she could invent a poem as easily as you make a grocery list. They would have burned them. And nothing ever ran from her, nothing innocent."

Lou came in softly. "I remember myself how the children used to follow her."

Now it was Al who spoke. "Then what reason did John and Jen have for treating her the way you claim they did?"

Victoria was too far into her angry grief to stop. "They couldn't stand the light that was in her."

Al looked suddenly burdened. He turned away. "Too much for me. I've work to do."

Lou put out her hand to touch Victoria but she sidestepped the gesture. "I don't understand you." The older woman sighed. "I'd like to but I can't."

Tuppenny handed Victoria the bag of lunch. "Come" was all she said, and to Lou's surprise Victoria quietly followed her out. She and Al watched them cross the churchyard and go in the direction of the river.

CHAPTER
~✦ 13 ✦~

"Let's sit here," said Victoria, choosing a flat rock at the water's edge. "It's as close as I can get to Dorrie."

Tuppenny settled herself just a little behind the other girl. Victoria's head was outlined against the gathering tumble of charcoal clouds. She handed Tuppenny a sandwich and they ate. "The river. It's always hurrying," Victoria murmured. "Like me—senselessly."

A silence fell, as definite and immovable as a column of stone. Tuppenny put the reed flute to her mouth and a flickering of notes rose between them. Victoria listened to the alien music so intently she seemed locked within its eloquent strangeness, and when it ceased she began to talk as though her words were an extension of the melody. "I'm wondering about you," she said.

"What?"

"Why I talked to you in the first place, much less asked you to come with me here. No, not who you are. I don't care about that. I've stopped digging into people. But why do I want to tell you something I swore they'd have to cut me open to find out?"

Victoria stared intensely at her companion. Then a small smile flicked across her mouth. "I think your eyes just changed color—from green to violet."

Tuppenny looked toward the sky. "It's all that doing the changing."

The clouds were mounting now into towers of darkness, so close together it seemed a premature fall of night.

"Maybe," said Victoria. "Hers did that, too. Maybe that's why I feel I can trust you—because you're like Dorrie." Then she grinned at herself. "But I'm getting foolish. The storm is brewing in me, too, I guess, and this *is* where she died."

Victoria clasped her hands, one in the other, as if she held something precious. "But there is a beginning," she said. "You've been in the church, haven't you?"

Tuppenny nodded. "It's a terrible place," she said.

"It's worse than that." Victoria's eyes were distracted, as if seeing backward in time. "It's worse than that. Evil lives in it. Why no true cross? No pictures of saints, not even a stray angel or two?" Her mouth quirked upward. "Not that I'd recognize one if it stepped on me." An almost inaudible drumbeat of thunder sounded from behind the hills. Victoria's smile vanished. "He's afraid, John Mason is. Afraid and insane. He takes his pleasure in distorting people." The girl's voice was edged with hysteria. "Who do you think ruined my mother? Maybe she tried to resist him but he finally hypnotized her into believing she loved him and when the affair was over—and you can be certain it was very brief—he blackmailed my father into allowing him the power he has over this rotten town."

"But why did she turn against you?"

"She had no choice. He convinced her that one day when it was to my advantage I would betray her. She had to drive me out."

"And if you knew all this you had to run away." Tuppenny's words were spoken gently.

"Why didn't I stand and fight?" Victoria mocked herself in a bitter spill of laughter. "God knows. I guess I just didn't have the guts."

"And you have now?"

"I don't know but I have to try. I began to hate myself and that's sure death."

"But how will you fight back?"

Victoria had quieted now. Her eyes were thoughtful. "One thing he can't stand up to or endure—it's what he couldn't bear in Dorrie—is any suggestion of light or goodness. It curdles him." She grinned. "I'm partly wicked myself. I got knotted somehow or maybe I was a changeling." Her sudden flippancy seemed to be an attempt to control an inner turbulence. "But what John and Jen are makes me want to vomit." She was now so tense she was shivering. "They tried to force Dorrie to worship the opposite of what exists in a church—any church but theirs. They made her kneel to it, and when she struggled they beat her. When I think of what they did to Dorrie I could kill them!"

She stood up, her back to Tuppenny.

"But you didn't," said Tuppenny, "and you won't."

"No. I haven't the courage to take the consequences. But I've come back to try my damnedest."

The thunder, nearer now, crackled across the far fields. Victoria abruptly wrenched her body in a half circle to face Tuppenny. Her voice rose. Her eyes were fierce. "Don't you understand?" she cried. "Dorrie didn't take her own life!"

The words had no sooner left her mouth than she was running. Tuppenny caught her at the road and gripped her by the arm.

"I never meant to tell you! I never meant to tell anybody!"

A first sweep of raindrops scattered over her cheeks like tears. They seemed to still her distress, to quench her ferocity. "Come with me, will you?" she said. The rapid reversal of emotions weakened her tones to a kind of guarded sweetness. "I'm going home and I don't want to go alone. Please?"

For reply Tuppenny began to walk toward the Standing mansion with Victoria following.

When they were before the front door, Victoria spoke again, pleadingly as a child might in confronting a fear. "You know too," she said, remaining behind her companion.

It was Mrs. Bunch who appeared. She saw only Tuppenny. "But come in, child! Come in!" she exclaimed. "I've missed you. They told me you were working for the Herds." She reached out to pull Tuppenny into the house. Her arm dropped. "Oh, my God! Miss Victoria! You're alive!" She stepped back to allow them entrance. "I was one who believed you had been kidnapped."

"That's at least a respectable interpretation," said Victoria, her face tight with strain. "I imagine the gossip was less kind." She brushed past the housekeeper. "My mother here?"

As though summoned, Maud's silhouette appeared on the threshold of the living room. A great gasp came from her throat and then her figure hurtled across the space between her and her daughter and she half fell against the girl, clutching at her around the shoulders to keep upright.

Victoria tried to stiffen, to repulse the embrace, but as she felt the older woman begin to slip downward as though her knees had suddenly weakened, she supported her, instead, to the nearest chair.

Maud breathed in gulps of air, never releasing her hold on her daughter. Victoria remained still until she quieted, then gently unpried her mother's fingers from the material of her coat. She fixed her mouth into a smile and spoke. "But you spoiled my entrance, mother. I planned to fight my way in with a speech I began rehearsing before I left."

Maud seemed not to have heard. "Oh, your father will be so happy!"

"I doubt that" was Victoria's reply.

"Don't," said Maud. "Don't ever doubt it. He's missed you since the moment you disappeared."

"And you, mother? Have you been saving up all the meannesses you used to let out on me? Are you looking forward to spewing them out now that I'm back?" Victoria's tones contradicted the cruelty of her words.

Tuppenny moved out of the shadows so that Maud must become aware of her.

"Not since—" stammered the woman, appealing to Tuppenny to help her. "Not since—" But Tuppenny only shook her head and waited. Maud looked directly into her daughter's eyes. "Not since I realized what I had been to you. Oh, Victoria!" she cried. "I was jealous! Jealous of your strange beauty, your independence, the love your father gave you. I was sick with it. And I was afraid of what you knew about me."

Victoria turned away as though she could no longer endure the truth of this fervent confession. She remembered her father's habit of having a glass of brandy after dinner and found the bottle and glasses where they had always been. She poured herself a little and drank it. "I need this," she said. "I feel—I feel reversed—all my feelings turned inside out and showing."

At that moment Victor Standing rushed into the room. He seized Victoria and hugged her hard. "Lou phoned me you had come back to us!" he said, finally able to let her go. "I came as fast as I could!"

Victoria gazed first at her mother and then her father as if they were strangers. Then a new smile formed very small. "Then I really am the prodigal daughter!" she said, denying the tears that brimmed her eyes.

Victor, his voice hoarse, met the effort. "The fatted calf will have to be lamb roast," he said. "It's the day for it. Right, Maud?"

His wife nodded and Victoria burst into clear laughter.

Unnoticed, Tuppenny slipped from the house. She began to walk toward the church.

CHAPTER
❧ 14 ❧

It was Jen who answered the bell at the rear of the church where their living quarters fronted the river. After the first flick of surprise at seeing Tuppenny, she propped her foot against the door to keep the girl from pushing her way in and called to her husband. "John! Come here!" Then to Tuppenny she said, "What do you want?"

"I want to serve you."

On the last word John stood beside his wife at the now fully opened door. Their narrowness of face and figure, similar except for the minister's added height, didn't quite fill the opening, but the gloom of the interior seemed to match the blackness of their clothes, smearing their outlines.

"Did you hear that, John? She wants to serve us. A miserable little whelp like that! A tramp off the roads. Order her out!"

But instead of agreeing he extended his hand to the waiting girl. "Come in, my dear. You are welcome here. We must talk this over."

Tuppenny ignored his gesture but entered, forced to move awkwardly to one side to pass the astonished Jen.

"Show her into my study," he instructed his wife.

The oblong room was all gray. Walls, desk, chairs—all except the portrait behind the desk, done by the same hand as the paintings in the church, only this one was recognizable. It was John Mason, smiling. Tuppenny felt an involuntary shudder track up her spine.

The minister had seated himself before the mounds of paper that cluttered his desk, and Tuppenny noticed that they were all yellowed, as though they had stayed stacked precisely as now for a very long time, like abandoned props on an unused stage.

He picked up a pen, plucked a piece of paper from the pile nearest him, and looked upward at the waiting applicant. "I must have some statistics," he said. "How old are you? Where do you come from? What is your entire name? Those of your parents?"

She saw his fingers relax around the stem of the pen as though he had no intention of inscribing whatever she might tell him.

"Why is all that important to you?" Tuppenny asked.

The man's grin was a slash across his face, made bright only by the whiteness of his long teeth. "I shall then assume, shall I, that you have no family, you are on your own for whatever reason—perhaps an escapee from an orphanage—but that is neither my concern nor my interest. I would say this is all for the best. No one will exercise any responsibility toward you, either legal or personal. Am I correct?"

He accepted Tuppenny's further silence for agreement. "But you worked for both the Standings and the Herds, did you not? And for very brief periods. Weren't you satisfactory? Though I'd hardly anticipate your revealing any outstanding faults." He paused to snicker lightly. "Not likely at all."

Tuppenny looked momentarily toward the window, to the winding green of the river, to the sky that held no color but gray. "Josie is coming home again," she said with a quiet that was almost soundless.

"That so? Can't say I'm glad to hear it. I always advised them both, repeatedly, that they keep her with her kind. Better for them. Better for the community. And the Standings?" He seemed to relish his role as questioner, as he might enjoy teasing a sow bug with a stick.

Tuppenny looked long at him, he interpreting her graveness as timidity. She said the words slowly. "Victoria has returned."

At this all semblance of self-satisfaction fell away from him. He dropped the pen and seemed not to notice its rolling to the floor. "Jen!" he called. "Come here immediately! I want you to hear this!"

The door opened so abruptly Tuppenny knew she must have been listening all the while directly behind it.

"Victoria has come back!" He rose in one swiftness and stalked to the window. "That girl!" he gritted out. "That wild, wicked girl! She corrupted our Dorrie. She led her into wanton ways, she demonstrated to our innocent child practices of the sinful world." His voice grew stentorian. He might have been standing on his pulpit, his captive congregation before him.

His wife went to him and shook him twice. He turned, raised one arm like a hammer, then suddenly reverted to his former suavity. "We always blamed her for Dorrie's death. Didn't we, Jen?"

The woman nodded hurriedly.

"Well, I doubt that she stays very long. Probably after some of her father's money so she can continue to live her contrary way." He was now in front of his desk, very close to Tuppenny. He picked up a paperweight shaped like a snake and shifted it from one hand to the other. "She put you up to coming here?" he said in too loud a voice.

Seeing from the girl's expression that she intended no reply, he let the weight tumble from his hands. It struck Tuppenny's left anklebone. She gasped but did not move.

"Oh, I'm so sorry! Hurt you, did it?" Excitement pinked his cheeks.

He clenched his hands around her upper arms and squeezed. "I want the truth out of you, you little—little creature! Are you here to spy on us? Did Victoria Standing plan this? Did she bribe you to insinuate yourself into our household? Answer me!"

Tuppenny's stomach sickened at the pressure of his hands but her reply came in even, serene tones. "I came because I am needed here."

At this both he and his wife exploded into high cackles of laughter. "Another weird one!" Saliva splattered his chin. "Needed? Needed? What arrogance! What absolute idiocy! A nobody tells me I need her!"

When their amusement had subsided he shifted into severity. "Now listen to me, girl. I'll not repeat what I have to say. We'll take you in—after all, we are charitable people—and give you food and lodging, but if you report anything you see or hear in our house, anything, no matter how minor, you will be very sorry indeed. Understood? Maybe we do need you, but not as you might suspect. We follow our own ways under this roof."

Tuppenny nodded her consent.

John winked at his wife, "Then get the hobble, dear."

Tuppenny stood very still while, a few minutes later, Jen affixed a thin wire circle around both her ankles, connected together by a foot-and-a-half length that would keep her from moving any faster than a slow and careful walk.

"We'll remove this when we feel we can trust you. You can take it off, but if you do you'll regret it. You'll soon accustom yourself to it. Dorrie did. And if you do take it off, I'll replace it with chains. All for the sake of discipline."

Tuppenny's dignity did not waver.

"Now, Jen, we'll have supper. You eat with us but meat is forbidden to you. Makes the blood run too rich. And afterwards you'll clean up and then go directly to your room. It's in the attic."

The hour was just past midnight when Tuppenny heard the tiny, repeated whistle. She had been leaning against the single window of the peaked, roof room, gazing out into the night, regretting the absence of moon and stars, unable to receive sleep or even enough tranquillity to lie upon the mattress that was her bed.

She strained upward against the window and achieved the opening of a crack. The frosted air cut at her legs, but she did not notice it. The whistle was more distinct now and she knew for sure it was not a bird.

Then a familiar shape half emerged from the bushes bordering the grass plot. It was Victoria. Her arm beckoned her down and pointed toward the river below.

Tuppenny waved back, hoping the other girl could see her. Then she loosened the wires and stepped out of the hobble. She had forgotten the threat of chains. With the caution and pace of a sleepwalker, she tiptoed to the doorway and began the descent to the second floor, balancing as delicately as an animal in case any creak of the floorboards might betray her going.

She had just come to the second staircase, past the last door, when she caught their voices. Jen was speaking timorously. "I tell you, John, I'm afraid of that Victoria.

hasn't come back for money. She's like Dorrie was—
didn't care whether she even dressed properly, just so she
could have the run of the fields and the hills. Never even
wondered what other people might think of her."

Jen's voice was high with fear. "Do you know why she's
come back? I'm nearly afraid to say it out loud. She's come
to make us confess."

"Don't be a fool, Jen. She has no proof. The church was
empty as a coffin when it happened and Dorrie was gagged.
Victoria could only guess, and who's to believe the tales of
a slut like that?"

Jen was weeping; dry, hard gulps of breath seeming to
thud against the door. "That night, John, I knew you were
the Devil."

A husky laugh came from the man. "Not Our Master,
himself, Jen, but his first squire, his honored knight, his
champion. Now shut up or that girl will hear you!"

Tuppenny hugged the wall as she took the remaining
stairs, but when she was at last a part of the outer darkness,
she ran as though she were being pushed from behind,
stumbling and leaping, to the river.

There was Victoria, as certain as a tree, waiting for her.
For a moment she neither smiled nor spoke. She simply
stared at Tuppenny. "I don't know why" were her first
words, "but every time I see you I miss Dorrie more than
ever."

Then she tossed her head as if to eject the idea. "I want
your help," she said. "You've got to let me into the church
tonight. I'm going to pretend I'm Dorrie. We looked alike
and this dress is like one they made her wear."

Tuppenny noticed that Victoria was covered by a long,
brown robe.

"It belongs to Mrs. Bunch. I told her I was cold and

she lent it to me. But none of that is important. You're to hide in a back pew and when you hear me scream, don't show yourself. I need a witness. All right?"

Tuppenny nodded. Victoria smiled. "Dorrie never spoke unless she had to. I used to tell her she saved words so she'd have plenty for her poems. One last thing. If what happens turns against me, I'd like to thank you in advance. For your help and for what you are, though I've only my feelings to tell me what that means."

She paused, and in the interval the river seemed to speak for her.

"Ready?" she asked.

"Ready," said Tuppenny.

In three minutes Tuppenny was crouched down at the rear of the church and Victoria was stationed before the bare altar, her arms outstretched in the form of a cross. A shriek crescendoed from her throat. Then a scramble of footfalls and the minister and his wife appeared through the side entrance.

The voice from the altar was slightly higher than Victoria's own and less hurried. "I have risen from the river where my spirit cannot rest. I must be avenged before final peace resides within me. I must have justice. I accuse you of murder!"

Jen screamed over and over again. John slapped her fiercely across the mouth, jolting the sound out of her. "It's a trick!" he shouted. "A fraud! She was dead as a stone when we threw her in!" But his tones held the start of hysteria. He lunged toward the obscure figure.

A glint of light flashed from the long knife the phantom girl held high. "I'll slit you as surely as you slit me if you don't halt!" commanded the voice. "Tell it, John Mason, before God and the Devil! Admit you killed me! I knew saw the satanic rites with which you profaned this tation you call a church! I was the sacrifice!"

Jen was now dragging the minister backward. "John!" she choked. "It is Dorrie! It's God's judgment on you at last!"

"On me?" he yelled. "On me? You held her while I cut. Never meant to kill her—it was an accident!"

At the pitch of her strength, Jen pulled them both down on their knees, shrieking "Save us! Save us!"

The spectre vanished. As Victoria reached the side door, Tuppenny met her. "Come on!" whispered Tuppenny in a rush. "We've got to get out! They've gone crazy mad!" She shoved Victoria violently out the door. But as she moved to follow, John, with Jen clinging like a sack around his waist, grabbed for her and held on.

"You demon!" he cried. "I'll kill you twice!"

"No, John, no! It's the other one—Tuppenny. Let her go! Don't harm her!"

"She has to die!" the minister spat out.

Tuppenny fought her way free, scarcely feeling the long, bloody raking of his fingernails as they scraped down her bare legs in an effort to stop her. She raced for the river, then, realizing she was in full view of her pursuer, dashed for the cover of bushes. Once within the maze of leaves she zigzagged her flight, all the time just a few feet ahead of the maddened man.

For five minutes the two of them thrashed through the undergrowth, the branches and brambles whipping at their passage like scourges wielded by invisible demons.

Then, in desperation, she abandoned this precarious concealment and cut out for the river. And just as she reached its banks and clasped her hands together to dive, he threw her to the ground. He wrenched himself and his victim upright, his fingers encircling her throat.

Jen was kneeling by the rush of water in an attitude of prayer, but what issued from her lips was a babbling as incomprehensible as the river's gush upon the rocks.

His hold tensed tighter and tighter. Tuppenny's eyes closed; her breathing ceased. With a cry that penetrated the depths of the night, he cast her into the rough flow of the river. As she floated out of sight, a little fleet of gold and scarlet leaves surrounded her body.

At that instant Victoria, followed by Victor and Al, Lou and Maud behind them, burst upon them.

Victor and Al held John prisoner on both sides while the two women lifted Jen to her feet. There was no resistance in either of them, and they allowed themselves to be led away with no protest but a senseless mumbling of broken dialogue between them.

CHAPTER
◅ 15 ▻

Three days later no one even well acquainted with the town and its people would have found a difference from how it had always been, no one except the few who had lived through what Lou called "the days of Tuppenny." The minister and his wife had been taken to a mental institution many miles distant. They had confessed to causing the death of their daughter, but their minds were so severely disconnected from reality, the court had ruled against legal proceedings. They would finish out their lives watched and guarded.

Lou resented the first excited buzzing of gossip, but now this, too, had ended. And she had Josie.

"I tell you, Al, I'm so happy I could make the morning doughnuts out of pebbles and sell them."

Al grinned. "Yeah. And Josie is sure picking up the idea of things fast. And you know, Lou, I'd forgotten something about her."

"What?" she asked, lining up the coffee cups for the first customers.

"She's pretty."

Lou hid her answering smile. Josie really wasn't pretty, but their love and Al's new patience had made her content. And she hummed small tunes all day long that seemed to weave harmony around her family.

"Something new about you, too," Al went on.

"Besides all this?" Lou asked, including the café and the three of them.

"Yes. You sort of dream off every once in a while."

"I'm remembering Tuppenny."

Al's eyes saddened. "Me, too. But I'll say it again, Lou, like I have a hundred times. I don't believe she drowned. She just took off, figured this wasn't her kind of place. We dragged the river, we reported her disappearance three counties down."

"I know," said Lou thoughtfully. "But wouldn't she have said good-bye to all of us? She was a strange girl, never said much to anybody, but she loved us. That I'm certain of. And look how she helped. Not just you and me and Josie, but the Standings; and now we're rid of that wickedness we called a church. Wish they'd tear it down, every last stone. Hear Victor's going to construct a new one."

Al looked out the front window. "Well, Victor did have the inside cleared. He talked yesterday of making a town hall out of it, for meetings and dances and sales. Said Maud wants the job of redecorating."

"I expect Victoria will have her ideas about that," commented Lou. "She's artistic, or so Maud tells me. Came in yesterday to see Josie, asked me to call her Vicky. I was so surprised I knocked over the cake stand. Made her chuckle. First time since Tuppenny left I've heard her even come close to laughing."

Lou wiped the last of the washed dishes before she spoke again. "That Tuppenny. Didn't have anything but the clothes she stood up in."

At that moment the back door slammed and Josie ran into the café. Her hands held a bunch of autumn leaves as bright in the sunlight as petals of stained glass. She put them tenderly down on the center table.

Al filled a glass with water and set it by the bouquet, but it was Lou who placed their stems, one by one, into the water. "We'll keep them for her" was all she said before she turned to greet the first customers of the day.

And it was that same shining morning that I, Jessica, found Tuppenny again. Each day since the loss of her I had awakened with the coming of light, dressed and left the house so silently no one knew me gone. I had run swiftly down the road that led into the town and there, where the turnoff forked from the highway, I had waited, as still as the grass that grew under my feet. No one and nothing had disturbed my vigil. Or was it a vigil? Perhaps just a foolish kind of hoping. But I prayed she would come.

As I stood there alone, someone touched me on the shoulder. I turned. It was Tuppenny.

I didn't move, but a joy sang inside me so strong, so sure, I felt somehow unbound, released from that halt in my inner self that forced me to stammer. I would not stammer again.

The first words were hers. "I just wanted you to know I was free of what they saw, the choking and the river and what looked like death."

My throat ached with that same joy.

"I must say good-bye," she said. "But someday we will meet again."

My quick tears blurred her image, but my voice came clear. "I'll soon be grown up and you too. How will I know it's you?"

"You will know."

As if coming from far away, there was a light rush of wind.

I instinctively looked up into the sky for birds, but there were none. And when I looked down again the road was empty, empty except for something small that lay at my feet. It was the reed flute. I picked it up and tightened my hand around it. This was the talisman of my beginning.

*Gilly Ground was an orphan who just
wanted a little peace and quiet . . .*

Dorp
Dead

by Julia Cunningham
illustrated by James Spanfeller

To escape the difficult life in the orphanage, Gilly
spent as much time as he could in the abandoned
tower in the woods. It was peaceful there—and it
was there that he met the Hunter. Then, one day,
Gilly was placed in the foster home of Mr. Kobalt.
And Gilly thought he was trapped in a nightmare
come true.

An Avon Camelot Book   51458 • $1.95

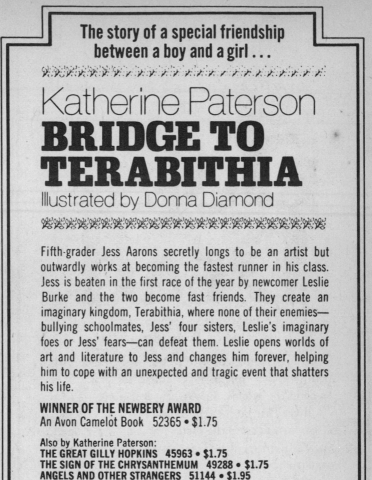